PHOBIA

Dr. T.K. Wheeler

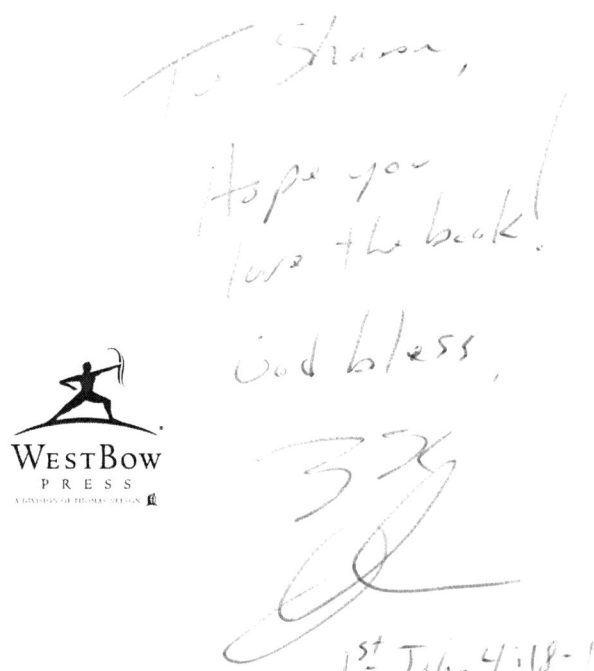

Copyright © 2013 Dr. T.K. Wheeler.

All rights reserved. No part of this book may be used or reproduced by any means, graphic, electronic, or mechanical, including photocopying, recording, taping or by any information storage retrieval system without the written permission of the publisher except in the case of brief quotations embodied in critical articles and reviews.

WestBow Press books may be ordered through booksellers or by contacting:

WestBow Press
A Division of Thomas Nelson
1663 Liberty Drive
Bloomington, IN 47403
www.westbowpress.com
1-(866) 928-1240

Because of the dynamic nature of the Internet, any web addresses or links contained in this book may have changed since publication and may no longer be valid. The views expressed in this work are solely those of the author and do not necessarily reflect the views of the publisher, and the publisher hereby disclaims any responsibility for them.

Any people depicted in stock imagery provided by Thinkstock are models, and such images are being used for illustrative purposes only.
Certain stock imagery © Thinkstock.

ISBN: 978-1-4497-8476-8 (sc)
ISBN: 978-1-4497-8478-2 (hc)
ISBN: 978-1-4497-8477-5 (e)

Library of Congress Control Number: 2013902582

Printed in the United States of America

WestBow Press rev. date: 2/15/2013

This one's for the boys: my nephews, Nicholas and Cal and my brothers-in-law, Robert and Steven.

There is no fear in love. But perfect love drives out fear, because fear has to do with punishment. The one who fears is not made perfect in love. We love because He first loved us.

1 John 4:18–19

Crrraaash!

The sound of the anvil hitting the door was like an unexpected boom of thunder on a summer afternoon. The doorframe splintered inward as the agents barged through the opening, rifles at the ready.

The tactical squad scattered in every direction possible, searching the house from room to room. One by one, each agent called out, "All clear!"

The team leader, Detective Jack Barnhill of the Atlanta Police Department, holstered his weapon as his men gradually worked their way back toward the living room of the modest one-story home. As the realization set in—their targets were not in the house—the unit looked to their captain for their next move.

Consternation etched itself across Jack's face. Something clearly was not right. No suspects. No weapons. *Were they tipped off to the raid?* he wondered. He rubbed his face in exhaustion and then doled out his directives to a more-than-eager battalion. "All right, guys, listen up. I want you to canvas every room one more time. This time we're gonna concentrate our search on the weapons. Cover the house from top to bottom. We need something out of here, fellas. Let's find it. Keep your guard up, and watch out for anything that doesn't look right. Okay, let's get to it. Be careful."

Jack still had an uneasy feeling in the pit of his stomach as his troops launched their second run through the house. His mind was abuzz with the possible reasons why they had come up empty on their first try.

As they searched, one of his men occasionally would call out that he had found something, like a small-caliber weapon or some type of ammunition. Regardless, these things weren't the specific targets they were after. One by one, the men began to trickle back into the living room again. Jack eyed each man who approached, clad in helmets, goggles, and black Kevlar stamped with APD in yellow, with weapons at the ready. Once they were all back, Jack drew them closer. "Good job, gentlemen," he said. "Unfortunately, this was not what we were led to believe it was. If nothing else, however, it was good practice for the real thing. We'll get 'em next time. All right, let's—" Jack stopped in mid-sentence. Everyone around him immediately snapped to attention, studying his face and body language. Lowering his voice to a whisper, he motioned to his second-in-command. "I didn't sweep this area," Jack said, pointing toward the coffee table and big-screen television.

Two agents sprang into action and started to sweep the area between the television and the wall. Jack anxiously watched. Thirty seconds later, one of the agents called out, "I've got something!" He motioned for one of the technicians to come over and inspect the device taped to the TV stand.

After several minutes of dismantling, examining, and finally disabling the small metallic box the technician mopped his brow with his glove and blurted out in relief, "It's not a bomb! It's a tiny surveillance camera. See this red light here, next to the black wire? That means it's on, and it's working---well, it *was* working. It's being run by remote control, but it's video only. It doesn't appear to have an audio component to it."

"So we were being watched," Jack said. "They knew we were coming?"

"Very possibly. Well, probably."

"Can you track where the remote signal might be coming from?" asked Jack.

"We can tap in through the camera wires, through the plug in the back, and hook in our own radar detector, which will give us the frequency of the signal from the remote. If they're still transmitting, and they're just a few miles from here, we can pick up the signal and pinpoint it to within a tenth of a mile."

"Do it."

The technician manipulated the lines running from the camera and added an attachment, strung it through, and plugged it into a handheld device that looked like a calculator with a video screen. He punched in a series of numbers that made the machine surge to life. The red, green, and yellow display exploded onto the screen and then finally slowed to a few lights and blips. After pressing the reset button, the device immediately stopped and a digital readout popped up.

The technician stared in disbelief. "This ca-ca-can't be right," he stammered.

"What is it?" Jack asked.

"Hold on just a minute." He readjusted the wires, made sure everything was calibrated correctly, and then pressed the reset button again. He explained the device to Detective Jack Barnhill. "When I press this reset key, it sends out a pulse that seeks the origin of the other signal. It can take up to ten minutes to hone in on the signal, depending on its intensity and frequency. Then it spits out the coordinates, and that's what these numbers indicate on the digital display. And ... I'm getting the *same* reading. No lag time at all. It's picking up the signal immediately!"

"So what's the reading?"

"It says the signal is coming from right here."

"Right here?" exclaimed Jack, causing the rest of the squad to snap back to attention.

"Somewhere within a two-hundred-yard radius of this house."

Jack's pulse raced as he pondered what his next move would be. He had to make a decision—and make it quickly. Suddenly, it came to him, and he voiced the command over the police radio. "We need backup on 854 Chestnut Oaks Drive. I need three square blocks cordoned off in each direction. Unknown number of suspects may be on the run. Over." *Chestnut Oaks Drive. Oaks! That's it!* He looked down at the floor in the living room. Hardwood floors made of oak. He looked up at the ceiling. Exposed beams overhead made of oak. "They're somewhere close by, gentlemen. This time we're gonna look high *and* low. Check all the floorboards for trapdoors or escape hatches and the ceilings for attic panels or pull-down ladders. Any hollow spots or dead spots you come across, double and triple check them. Okay, let's go."

The men scattered in pairs to each room, one searching the ceiling and the other tapping the floor. Jack watched the proceedings with a careful eye, hoping that his instincts were correct. He paced back and forth, watching his men and occasionally glancing out the window. Something strange caught his eye on one of his random glimpses. A few feet away, just outside the window, was an rotting oak tree, its top sheared off; a piece of the trunk, shaped like a crescent moon, was missing. At the bottom of the trunk, Jack's keen eye noticed what he believed to be a patch of spilled concrete. He grabbed one of the men from the unit and stepped in front of him. Unholstering his weapon, Jack growled for the agent to follow him.

They moved in tandem out the front door, down the steps, and over to the tree. Detective Barnhill reached down with his left hand and scratched the ground near the trunk of the tree. His instincts were right—it was a small blob of concrete. Reholstering his weapon, Jack dropped to his hands and knees and swept his palms across the dirt area in wide arcs, drawing curious looks from his partner and a few other members of the unit who had migrated outside. He gradually uncovered more concrete and steel, working faster as he did. Several more quick sweeps up and down confirmed his suspicions—it was a manhole cover. But what was it doing inside a hollowed-out tree trunk?

"Gimme a hand with this, will ya?" Jack motioned to a couple of the men standing nearby.

A hydraulic lift was quickly carted over from a nearby police van as the men rushed forward to aid Jack. Positioning the thin jack under the manhole cover, one of the squad members pressed the handle of the power lift until the lid lifted slightly. Barnhill grabbed it, shoved it aside, and shined his flashlight into the blackness.

Well-worn metal rungs were bolted to the wall, leading down into a twenty-foot hole. The tactical squad checked their headlamps, readying themselves for a possible descent into the narrow cavity. Jack drew in a long breath. "Guys" he said slowly, "I think this could be a concrete bunker." The men began to murmur as they awaited their orders. Without hesitation, Jack withdrew his firearm and started down the opening.

"Jack! Jack! Wait!" his second-in-command whispered harshly.

"C'mon," Jack said. "We're wasting time!"

One by one, the men quickly fell into line as they followed their leader into the dark hole. Jack tiptoed down the ladder rungs until he reached the hard concrete floor at the bottom. He spun around, gun drawn, his flashlight slashing through the darkness. As his eyes adjusted to the endless black tunnel in front of him, Jack slowly crept forward, allowing the other men to drop in behind him. Their headlamps shone from the back, gradually illuminating their way.

A few more feet down the hallway, the dim light flickered on a small door just to the left. Jack waited for all the men to join him beside the door. Collecting himself, he took a deep breath and studied the entrance. He tested the door handle—it was unlocked!

Peering back at the men, Jack held up his fingers and began a silent count to three. As he led the charge through the door, Jack was both intense and in awe when the scene in front of him finally registered in his brain. It was almost as if they had stumbled into an illegal gun shop. From floor to ceiling, weapons were lined up, stacked up, and boxed up in crates—AK-47 assault rifles. Israeli-made Uzis. German-made H and K G36s. TEC-9s. Colt AR-15s. This was the mother lode of assault-weapon caches. He glanced over to a far corner of the room, where a younger man, apparently a guard and no more than twenty years old or so, was just stirring from slumber. In an instant he found himself thrown to the ground, face down, with several weapons from the tactical team shoved in his face.

He's the only fish on the hook for now, Jack thought, *but it takes a little fish to catch a bigger fish. We just need to be patient.*

Three days later, it would pay off. He and his men, in conjunction with the FBI, ATF, and Department of Homeland Security, would conduct a sting that uncovered a huge international illegal weapons trading ring. The sting eventually would lead to hundreds of arrests, and aid them in the recovery of hundreds of millions of dollars in cash and weapons. A nice catch, indeed.

2

The sound of boots being pulled up flight after flight of stairs was not exactly the sound one might associate with small-town America. The jingle of spurs or the clomp of soles and heels against a wooden floor served as background noise to everyday life in this part of the world but not this specific noise. It was odd enough in its nature, but even stranger that no one was around to hear it. Twentysomethings and those who still wished they were that age were moving from place to place, looking for fun and friendship, even in a town as tiny as Valley Springs. Plenty of people were out on this particular Saturday night. Someone should have heard the noise. Yet no one did.

It probably would have been much easier to throw the girl over his shoulder and carry her that way, rather than dragging her by draping his arm under her arms. Sure, she was dead weight, but she couldn't have been much more than one hundred pounds, soaking wet. But with all of the auxiliary equipment he was hauling, there was no other alternative than to drag her. Either way, it wasn't an easy climb. Even someone in top physical condition would have had a tough time pulling off the logistics this exercise entailed. The abandoned fire tower once used by Forestry Services loomed like a sentinel in the late-night darkness. Fourteen stories. Eight steps between each story. One hundred twelve steps, straight up. It took him fifteen minutes to scale the entire structure. After a few seconds to catch his breath, the real fun would begin. A thin line of sweat trickled down the middle of his back, causing his shirt to cling tightly against his torso. He was dressed all in black, from fingertips to ankles, except for the light blue shoe covers he wore to avoid leaving footprints. Reaching down into the equipment bag, he produced a miner's headlamp, a carabiner clip, and a long extension of nylon rope. A quick glance assured him of the victim's continued state of unconsciousness. She faced upward, as if in a deep slumber, looking no worse for wear except for the scuff marks on the heels of her shoes. He had chosen her carefully after weeks of surveillance. He'd crept into her house, knocked her out with chloroform, injected her with the ivory-colored opaque solution, and quietly stuffed her into his car. He knew her strengths but more important, he knew her weaknesses, her fears. Now was the time to expose them to the world.

The man slipped on the headlight, knelt down beside her, and extracted a roll of duct tape from the black bag. He made several revolutions, first around her ankles and then around her wrists. He threaded the rope behind her back, down through the small gap between her wrists and the tape, and through the tape on her ankles. Tying one end of the nylon to the carabiner, he hooked the other end around the window frame. He dug into the black bag again and pulled out a syringe containing a clear liquid and a small index card. Quickly tearing off a small piece of duct tape, the man taped the index card to the carabiner and hoisted the girl up and out of the window. She dangled by her feet, high in the air, like a newly caught fish. She was still unconscious, but that would soon change. Gathering up everything and shoving it into the bag, he slung it over his shoulder and then carried out the last detail of his intricate plan. The man leaned over the side of the fire tower and injected the clear liquid into the girl's right calf muscle. He pulled out the needle, capped it, and popped it into the bag. Swiftly making his way back down the stairs, he figured that he had about five minutes before the drug kicked in and brought her back to consciousness. His assessment was dead-on accurate. Just a few feet from the bottom, the man heard a blood-curdling scream above his head. The full-throated shrieks continued as he threw the bag into the SUV and sped away. Picking up his cell phone, which he'd fitted with an encryption device and a voice modifier, he placed a 9-1-1 call to the police to let them know about his handiwork.

"9-1-1. What is the nature of your emergency?"

"I'd like to report a female impersonating a pendulum."

"I'm sorry, sir. Can you repeat that?"

"There's a young girl swinging by her feet from the top of the old fire tower, and she doesn't seem too happy about it."

"Sir, can you tell me—"

The man suddenly broke into song, interrupting the operator. "I believe I can fly. I believe I can touch the sky."

"Sir? Sir!"

"Tinker Bell is gonna be ticked off!" he whispered just before abruptly hanging up the phone.

"Hello? Hello, sir? Are you there?"

The dispatcher sent two patrol cars, and within a matter of minutes, they were barreling toward the tower. Skidding to a stop on the makeshift gravel and dirt road, the patrolmen leapt from their squad cars, eyes pointed skyward. In the shadows of a quarter moon, they could see the body dangling from a rope near the top of the structure. The men made a mad dash from their cars to the base of the stairs, just underneath the bottom ledge. As they tried to catch their breath, one of the officers snatched his flashlight from his utility belt and shined the light upward to investigate.

"Hello!" he shouted between gasps. "Can you hear me?" The officer did not get a response. He could only hear the sounds of his own blood rushing through his ears and the wheezing of his partner, who was staring into the night sky and trying desperately to breathe deeply.

Once both men had caught their second wind, they plodded up several more flights of steep steps, pausing along the way to listen for anything strange. *What is that noise…and where is it coming from?* the first officer asked himself. A millisecond later, it dawned on him. *Someone's hyperventilating…from up there!* He pointed his flashlight up and shouted toward the victim. "Just hold on! We're coming up to help you! We're on our way! Calm down! Breathe! Relax and breathe! We're coming!" *Easy for me to say,* he thought. *I'm not hanging fourteen stories in the air by my ankles.*

The two officers bounded up the final few flights of stairs, the gasping and wheezing of the victim piercing their eardrums. The lead officer kept his eyes on the twisting body, while the trailing officer feverishly called for backup. With every step, every landing, every flight of stairs, their legs grew heavier. Their labored breathing shattered the soundless night, making it nearly impossible to distinguish their own puffing from the victim's. By the time they approached the thirteenth story, both men felt as if their lungs would explode, so they stopped for a moment. As they rested briefly, the officers looked up at the body. The woman's screaming had stopped. Now she appeared to be literally twisting in the wind. The first officer pointed his flashlight at the body, which was just a few feet away. The light cast a glow on the girl's face, further emphasizing the whiteness of her eyes—the unblinking, lifeless, pale stare of her eyes. The sight jolted the officers back into action and sent them bounding up the last few steps. Bursting through the tower's door, the men ran over to the window, grabbed the rope, and pulled with all their might. As they hauled the body back over the edge and into the tower, they could hear the distant sound of police, fire, and other emergency personnel arriving on the scene and bouncing their way up the stairs.

As the lead officer began CPR, the other gave radio updates on the girl's condition. Within fifteen minutes, everyone in town knew. As the second wave of responders made their way into the tower, the two patrolmen had stopped compressions and just stared at the others in exhaustion.

"That's it, guys. She's gone."

$$\Omega$$

The crime was the biggest thing to hit Valley Springs since the new restaurant opened out on Highway 28. People couldn't stop buzzing about it. Some enterprising souls even tried in vain to cash in on the crime scene after the Crime Scene Unit had completed all of its work, but the entrepreneurs were dismissed by some of Valley Springs' finest.

Meanwhile, the girl's body had been transported to the morgue, and the autopsy was well underway. The county's medical examiner, London Brown, was walking Valley Springs Chief of Police Wyatt Hart through his findings.

"And if you look here, down toward the back of her throat, you'll see that she had bilateral hemorrhaging of the vocal cords, probably caused by her screaming."

"You mean screaming caused her throat to fill with blood, and that's what killed her?" questioned Chief Hart.

"Not really, though that didn't help matters. She apparently died of heart failure," said Dr. Brown.

"Heart failure?"

"Yes, take a look at this." The medical examiner walked over to a side table where a file folder had been flipped open and bookmarked on two particular pages. He pulled off his latex gloves, tossed them into the garbage bin, and pointed at the left side of the folder. "Our victim had no other previous medical history until just a few years ago, when she was diagnosed with a certain type of anxiety disorder." Chief Hart gave a quizzical look as Dr. Brown continued. "She was on medications for acrophobia, a fancy way of saying she was afraid of heights. According to this, even one flight of stairs was enough to freak her out."

"Really?"

"Apparently so."

"So imagine how a fourteen-story fire tower would make her feel."

"Exactly."

"What did the tox screen indicate?"

"It's due back any minute."

"Let me know as soon as you get it," the chief said. "What about the rest of the evidence?"

"We couldn't get anything from the index card. All we know is that this guy is trying to make a point, but he's not stupid. He left no fingerprints. He used index cards you can get anywhere. Bottom line is, he's virtually untraceable at this point. We've got nothing on him."

Chief Hart rubbed his face in fatigue and frustration. "Just great. And all we have to go on is this cryptic message that doesn't make sense. I have no idea what it's supposed to mean."

Before Dr. Brown could respond, his assistant burst through the swinging double doors, waving the toxicology report. "London, wait until you see this," the medical assistant exclaimed.

3

The crowd at the press conference was nearly suffocating. The conference room's capacity was only twenty people or so, but there were at least three times that many present. The local media was there as always, but on this particular day, members of the national press were in attendance. Normally, the story would have held no interest beyond the area newscast, but this weapons bust had made headlines all across the country, simply because of the monetary value involved. The small stage set up in the back of the room was a study in opposites. On the left side of the podium were the politicians, grinning from ear to ear, as if they'd actually taken part in the sting. The mayor. The city council chairwoman. The area ATF and FBI bureau chiefs. They truly loved the attention and were warmly basking in the TV lights. The men on the right half of the dais rather would have been anywhere but there. The chief of police. The head of Tactical Operations. Detective Jack Barnhill. All the law enforcement officials saw this as unnecessary—a three-ring circus that didn't need to be performed. They'd done their job. What was so special about that?

The mayor finally stepped forward and waved his arms in the air to get the crowd noise under control. Gradually, the chattering subsided, and he began the introductions. "Good afternoon. I want to thank you all for coming today. First of all, I'd like to introduce everyone here on the platform. After they make their remarks, we'll open it up for questions." The mayor then went through the tedious task of identifying each person, spelling the name for the press, and elaborating on the job titles for each. All of the politicians prattled on about how great the other agencies were in helping capture the suspects and recovering the weapons. Finally, questions were directed to those in law enforcement. These kinds of press conferences were precisely why they preferred to work behind the scenes, behind a desk, or undercover—they embraced their anonymity. Despite the awkwardness of the moment, they realized that the media had a job to do as well, so they respected that and grudgingly endured the tired clichés and dumb questions as best as they could. As the inquiries slowly drew to a close, a reporter from National News Network asked the lawmen if they had received any special commendations or if any of the federal agencies had given out a reward.

"Well, if they decide to give out a reward, I suppose I'd have to take it," cracked the chief of police. "I wouldn't want to hurt their feelings." That sent the room into an uproar of laughter. "In all seriousness, that money would end up going to everyone in our department, so that's not so bad. Personally, I'd be happy with a citation … and maybe a day off."

After the laughter had subsided, the head of Tactical Operations spoke up. "We do a seven-day-on/seven-day-off schedule, so I'm at the end of my workweek. I'm looking forward to the week off. All I want to do is spend time with my wife and kids. That's reward enough for me."

Lastly, Detective Jack Barnhill chimed in. "Since I don't have much longer before I retire, I need some extra time off. I've gotta figure out what comes next for me. I'm sure my wife will have something to say about where we end up, but a week or two to get our retirement plans together would help out. Anyone got a condo in Florida for sale?"

After posing for a few more photos, the press conference wound to a close as the groups on the stage made their way to a private area away from the popping flashbulbs and the glare of the television lights.

Gradually, the mayor wormed his way through the crowd and called out to the police chief. "Jerry, I need to see you and your men, ASAP."

"You mean right now?"

"If that's okay."

"Sure, let's go over to my office."

The four men crossed the main reception area and ducked into the chief's tidy but cramped office. Jack grabbed a couple of chairs from the break room and dragged them into the office.

The mayor was the last one to arrive, closing the door behind him. "Gentlemen," he began, "I just wanted to let you know personally what an excellent job your men did, especially you three in particular. You made Atlanta look great in the national spotlight. I also know you guys well enough to know that's not why you do what you do. You're not about the glory. You're about getting it done and getting it done the right way. You were technically sound, played your hunches, and knocked it out of the park. I want you to know that this mayor appreciates you and all the great work that you do. So here's what I'm thinking: even before the media onslaught out there, I was already brainstorming about what I could do for you guys. I've decided that each of you will get an extra week off with pay, a separate commendation ceremony and reception from the city of Atlanta, and depending on how much filters down from the Feds, you'll get a small monetary reward. How does that sound?"

"An extra week off with pay? Sounds great to me!" exclaimed the Tactical Operations Head.

"Thank you, sir. That's more than generous," the chief said.

"Thank you, Mayor. The extra week off will come in handy," Detective Barnhill gushed.

"You guys will probably want to hang out around here until Thursday or so, just to deal with any more of the press still straggling around in search of a story. As soon as they hit the road and your individual schedule permits, you've got my approval to take off for the week. You might want to keep your cell phones on in case we need to get in touch with you, but I honestly don't see that happening. Once again, congratulations on a job well done. You have made your families and the rest of the city proud of you. Good day, gentlemen."

The three officers rose from their chairs and shook hands with the mayor as he departed the office. Deep inside, they were thrilled at the prospect of a week's paid leave. The tactical operation itself had not been particularly grueling, but the ensuing days after the takedown were a blur of bureaucracy and never-ending paperwork. Documenting every weapon, every action taken, and every officer involved was truly an exercise in tedious grunt work. As the mayor disappeared, the three men let their guard down.

"Do you believe this?" the chief questioned. "The mayor actually did something *for* us for a change."

"Miracles never cease," joked Barnhill.

"Jack, you and Steven get your hides out of here. We'll see you tomorrow."

"Thanks, Chief. See you in the morning."

$$\Omega$$

The next day, during a rare moment of downtime from the media onslaught, the three men met together to briefly discuss the order in which they would take their paid vacation week. It was decided that since the head of Tactical Operations was heading into his off week, he would wait until week two. This would give him three straight weeks off. Perfect. Detective Barnhill was the elder statesman of the three, had the most seniority, and had the best excuse to take a vacation now. After all, retirement wasn't too far away, so he would take his vacation time first. As the leader and figurehead of the weapons operation, the chief of police would do the noble thing and go on week three. "If only all decision making and negotiations were as easy," the chief smiled.

$$\Omega$$

Jack and Heather Barnhill sat at the kitchen table after polishing off bowls of homemade vegetable soup that had been simmering in the Crock-Pot. The Barnhills had been married for nearly thirty-five years. They'd grown up in the same hometown, attended the same schools, knew the same people, and had all the same friends. Most of the time, they could finish each other's thoughts. So it was no surprise what both of them were thinking when the retirement topic raised its head.

"Have you been praying about it?" Jack inquired.

"I have, and do you know what I think?" Heather replied.

"Sure I do, but humor me, and tell me anyway," he said as a slight grin nudged his face.

"We've wandered in the wilderness, so to speak, for nearly forty years. Washington DC. Atlanta. I love them both, but now I know for sure that there's no place like home. Valley Springs is the place for me. It's the place for *us*. We've done the fame and fast-lane thing. Let's go sit on a front porch in our rocking chairs, sip some sweet tea, listen to the sounds of the crickets chirping, and breathe in the fresh air for the rest of our days."

"No second thoughts? No Orlando or Naples or Scottsdale or Palm Springs?"

"Nope. I feel like the Lord's in this. It's time for the prodigal son ... and daughter ... to go home."

Jack broke into a mile-wide grin. "I was hoping you'd say that."

The two embraced each other for a few seconds and then set out to make plans for their homecoming trip to Valley Springs. "Since I've got this vacation time coming up, why don't we just drive down there and stay the week?" said Jack.

"We can go down, get reconnected with some of our old friends, and let them know that we're coming back home to stay. It'll be great!" replied Heather.

"Yeah, get away from the city; relax a little bit. We'll have plenty of time to hang out and look at some real estate, too. You know, see if we want to buy a house or build our own."

"Oh, Jack. I'm so excited!"

"Me, too, babe. Me, too."

The two began to get emotional and hugged each other once again. After Jack swallowed the lump in his throat, he leaned down and whispered into Heather's ear. "Who says you can't go home again?"

Ω 4

The police chief of Valley Springs and the county medical examiner peered up in anticipation of the assistant's news.

"What does it say?" Dr. London Brown inquired of his lab assistant.

"Tox screen shows levels of both alprazolam and lorazepam to be within normal limits," the assistant enthusiastically said.

"So why wouldn't I believe that?"

"That's not the fun part. Those are her maintenance medications. It's the other drugs I found that will pique your curiosity."

"Okay …"

"Abnormally high levels of midazolam *and* epinephrine," the assistant reported.

"Midazolam and epinephrine? Help me out here, bud. I don't see the connection."

"Right. You'd think those two drugs would balance each other out."

"Someone want to tell *me* what's going on here?" Chief Hart interjected, somewhat indignantly.

Dr. Brown's face flushed with embarrassment. "Oh, yeah," he said. "Midazolam is a benzodiazepine, similar to the alprazolam and lorazepam that the deceased was taking. Basically, it is used to cause relaxation or sleep. We usually don't see this medication unless a person was about to undergo a surgical procedure. It helps in putting the patient to sleep and in blocking memories of the surgery."

"So … it's almost like a knockout drug?"

"Yes, but it's legal by prescription and widely used in hospital settings everywhere."

"What about the epinephrine? How does that factor into this?" the chief asked.

The medical assistant quickly piped up in response. "Well, since the effects of midazolam can last for several hours after injection, the epinephrine was probably used to wake her up speedily."

"But why would you inject her with both? Aren't they antagonistic of each other?" asked Chief Hart.

"I don't think our guy was trying to kill her with the drugs, or he'd have done her in with the midazolam—just knocked her out and left her for dead," Dr. Brown reasoned.

"I'm thinking our perp plays on the fears of these women, letting their own personal fears kill them," the chief suggested. "He injects them with midazolam to knock them out and then sets up their … their phobia by waking them up in the middle of it. One giant dose of epinephrine and … let the games begin."

"Instant panic! Instant heart attack! Chief, I believe you nailed it," replied Dr. Brown.

"Let's keep this under our hats until we figure out what the index card means and how it relates to this case," the chief said.

The index card had been left intentionally at the crime scene, a calling card of sorts. It was very ordinary in its appearance, except for one thing. Right in the middle of the card was an omega symbol in red ink, with the words **FACE YOUR FEARS** printed in bold lettering just underneath.

$$\Omega$$

The small room was ten feet by ten feet, slightly larger than a walk-in closet, with doors on either end. The man had hauled the chair into the abandoned house and through the first door. After tipping the chair onto its back, he reached around the doorframe and grabbed a small metal tank, the kind usually used by pest exterminators. The man opened up the nozzle and began to spray a chemical pheromone from floor to ceiling. He started at the first door, worked his way over the woman's body, and then made his way out of the second door. Retracing his steps, the man paced back toward the unconscious woman. He then pulled a syringe from his pocket, uncapped it, and injected the woman with a large dose of epinephrine. Making his way back toward the rear exit, he produced a large container he'd brought from outside and launched its contents in front of the door.

They were so small that they hardly made a sound, but they were like a tiny marching army—a very creepy tiny marching army. Stop and go. Stop and go. This was the stuff of science fiction movies or a bad horror film. The young housewife lying on the floor didn't seem to notice their machine-like motion. *Kind of hard to notice anything when you're duct taped to a chair, flipped over onto your back, and half-full of benzodiazepines*, he thought. The spiders were on the move, and they were everywhere. These were not your ordinary pet shop tarantulas, nor were they the deadly poisonous black widows or brown recluses. Just thousands and thousands of long-legged spiders. It was only a matter of seconds before the woman became totally aware of her surroundings. The huge dose of epinephrine notwithstanding, her heart became electrified, nearly pounding out of her chest. Her eyes bulged from their sockets and darted from side to side as the insects made a pheromone-fed beeline for her. She tried to wriggle free, but the duct tape held strong. Her whimpering only seemed to push the spiders closer and closer. Screaming would do her no good. Her mouth was sealed tightly with more of the silvery, sticky tape. Then, as if hit by a bolt of lightning, a reality struck her heart and mind with a blinding truth. She was all alone. Held as a captive who-knows-where and covered in duct tape like a cheap piece of furniture. Thousands of spiders creeping toward her, and she couldn't move! Her thoughts and fears started to spiral, until they set off a full-fledged panic attack. Her body began to jerk and twitch as the pheromone-driven creatures made their way into her hair, down her forehead, into her ears, and in the direction of her eyes, nose, and mouth. They had become so numerous on her face that she had to force her eyes closed. The woman's throat had become so raw from screaming through the tape that she winced with every breath.

Her muscles had rapidly fatigued—that must be the tingling she felt—in her futile tries at up-righting the chair in which she sat. Or maybe it was the tiny, hairless legs making their way across the rest of her body. At this point they had crossed over to both of her arms and legs and covered most of her neck and torso. A few adventurous crawlers had even taken a stab at entering her nostrils but were rebuffed by her labored breathing. Someone walking in on the scene might wonder how anyone could have been hidden under such a gigantic mass of spindly legs. Yet there she was, buried alive by spiders. As the last pangs of panic washed over her, the housewife felt a squeezing around her chest and clenched her eyes even tighter. Not long afterwards, her breathing rapidly sped up and then slowed down just as quickly. Then, everything in her world went black.

$$\Omega$$

The man briskly made his way to the late-model SUV, slipped in the keys, and cranked the motor to life. He glanced down at the modified cell phone lying in the passenger's seat and started to pick it up when he noticed something making its way down his right arm. *Stupid spider*, he thought as he reached over with his left hand and crushed the long-legged critter, flicking it from his shirt with his thumb and middle finger. Once his extermination duties were carried out to his satisfaction, he jerked the car into gear and headed down the highway. No regrets. No remorse. No conscience. The next part of his plan was the most fun for him personally—the 9-1-1 call. He picked up the electronically altered phone from the passenger's side and initiated communications. One ring. Two rings.

"9-1-1. What is the nature of your emergency?" came the voice of the dispatcher.

"Um … yes, operator. A friend of mine seems to be having some kind of … pest control issue."

"I'm sorry, sir. Can you repeat that?"

"I could, but I really don't feel like it. I like the way I said it the first time. Your loss. However, I think I can put it in another way that you will better understand."

"Sir, are you okay? Your voice seems a bit … strained or garbled."

"It's probably this voice modifier I'm using, but I'm not the point here. Let's focus on why I called. Let's focus on my friend."

"Okay, sir. Calm down, and tell me what's wrong with your friend."

"Well, I will if you'll shut up and stop interrupting me! Honestly, where did you learn your manners? Your mom and dad apparently didn't raise you right!"

There was a long pause before the operator responded again. "Go ahead, sir."

"Now, as I was saying before I was so rudely interrupted, I have a female friend … we'll call her Little Miss Muffett, who's flat on her back right now. She seems to be really 'bugged' about it." After another long pause, the man spoke once more. "Okay, last time I'm going over this, so pay attention!" The man cleared his throat and proceeded to sing. "The itsy-bitsy spiders crawled up the poor housewife. If your men don't hurry, she's gonna lose her life. Forty-seven fourteen Old Plantation Drive is where you're gonna find her; that's if she's still alive." The end of his nursery rhyme done, the man clicked off the cell phone.

The dispatcher frantically tried to trace the call and simultaneously send out patrol cars to the possible crime scene. Minutes later, first responders burst through the front door at the abandoned ranch-style home. The police and other rescue personnel bolted through the interior rooms, spiders crunching underfoot as they progressed through the house. They had cleared all but two rooms in the rear of the home when they stumbled upon a large lump in the center of the first room. Only when their flashlights shone against the metal chair did they realize they'd found her. Buried underneath hundreds of spiders was the unidentified female they'd been sent here to find. Victim number two.

5

The time had finally come. Jack and Heather had their bags packed for almost a whole week before they were scheduled to leave. Now that day had arrived. This day felt to them like the old bumper sticker that read *"Today is the first day of the rest of your life."* Jack had gassed up the Suburban, and after a quick home-cooked breakfast, he and Heather set off for Valley Springs. Normally, they would have been sad to see the Atlanta skyline disappearing in their rearview mirror but not today. Both of them were ready to get away from all the attention, to enjoy each other's company, and just hang out with lifelong friends back in their old hometown. Everywhere they looked along the route home seemed to jar latent memories buried deep within their minds, things they'd seemingly forgotten years ago—the old barbecue restaurant that was still a local institution. The roadside fruit and vegetable stands. The military base, survivor of so many military cutbacks made by Congress over the years. The same speed-trap towns with the police hiding in the same old spots. Some things never changed. Time seemed to have frozen in this part of the South. Oh sure, there was the occasional new convenience store or remodeled antique shop, but for the most part everything had been left just as they had remembered it. And that was just how they liked it.

As their car concluded its nearly four-hour journey and rolled to within thirty miles of Valley Springs, Jack reached down and clicked on the radio. He grinned. "Let's get some local flavor. It'll get us in that Valley Springs state of mind."

"Wonder if AM 880 is still around," Heather said.

"And this has been your daily farm report. We'll be back with the fish and game report right after these important messages on your voice of the South, WCVC-AM 880."

Heather and Jack glanced at each other and almost immediately burst into laughter. After three local advertisements for an insurance company, a car dealership, and a hardware store, the bumper music trickled through the stereo speakers as the talk-show host returned to the airwaves.

"Today, we're going to suspend the fish and game report, as well as the rest of our regular programming to take calls from you, our local listeners. There are many out there who are scared—and understandably so. There are a lot of rumors and misinformation floating around, so we want to be here for you and talk you through it. We have not heard anything new from the authorities, and there aren't likely to be many answers forthcoming."

Jack and Heather's eyes widened. What was this? What was happening in Valley Springs? Jack edged the radio volume up just a bit as the host continued.

"We're gonna take a few calls. We know you need to talk this out, so let's try to keep a level head as best as we can. Let's go to Sandra. Sandra, you're on WCVC."

"Hello?"

"Go ahead, Sandra. You're on the air."

"Yes, I heard that the second victim's body had been assaulted and later, her extremities were cut off. Have you heard that?"

"No, ma'am. We have not heard that and frankly, I don't think that's true. The police would have said if the deceased had been hacked up, if for no other reason than to warn us to lock our doors. As far as the assault, who knows? At this point, they're treating each case as a separate yet unrelated murder, until they can tie them together."

"Murder!" Jack and Heather shrieked at the radio in unison.

"Let's go to line four. Go ahead, caller. What's your name and your question?"

"Hello, this is Hilda in Valley Springs. I am a widow, living alone on the outskirts of town. This is just awful and truly terrifying for me, personally. It seems to me that we have a serial killer in our *own* hometown, but no one wants to acknowledge or admit it. Why won't the police say something ... anything along those lines? I think most people would rather know than not know."

"Well, Hilda, in a town as small as we are, not everyone is gonna be logical. This kind of thing doesn't happen in Valley Springs every day. This happens in Atlanta, in New York, in Los Angeles, in Chicago. Not here. It's not the norm, so people are trying to cope with it as best as they can. Unfortunately, some people do that by causing a panic or an uproar among the citizens here. All we can do is keep calm, stay alert, lock our doors, and try to look out for each other. Call your friends and neighbors to make sure they're okay, but *please* don't call the police for updates. As you can imagine, they've got their hands full and don't need to be tied up with individual reports. I'm sure they'll catch this monster, so just let them do their jobs. To answer your question, I don't think you can call it the work of a serial killer just yet, despite the odd coincidence of two murders that close together chronologically. However, if they can link the two cases, I'm sure the big-city media machine will be more than happy to let us know. Right now, that's the last thing anyone in our community needs."

Jack and Heather sat in stunned silence through the rest of the segment until the next commercial break.

"Who said some things in a small town never change?" Heather said. "Do you ever recall anything like this happening in Valley Springs?"

"Never! Plenty of deaths. Old age. Heart attacks. Strokes. Cancer. But murder? Never!" exclaimed Jack.

"Isn't our buddy still the chief of police?"

"Yes, and I was going to try to pay him a surprise visit, but I don't think he'll have time for me now."

"Well, you never know ..."

"Trust me; he's way too busy. Besides, he might get offended if I show up uninvited and start nosing around in his case."

"You guys *are* still friends, right?"

"Yes, but it's professional courtesy to keep your nose out of someone else's business unless he asks for your help. He may think I'm trying to 'big city' him a little bit."

Heather nodded. "I'm sure we'll eventually run into him. We've got a whole week to get reacquainted with basically everyone from our childhood days." She glanced up just as they whizzed by a sign that read *Valley Springs 5 Miles*. The talk-show host had come back from commercial break and started to take more phone calls, but Heather spoke over the sound of his voice. "So where do we start our reunion tour?" she joked.

"Let's go check into the hotel, and then we'll work our way across town."

"Okay. That means the bank is the first stop. After that, the pharmacy, the café, the grocery store, the gas station, the florist, the church office, and then the police station. We'll make a big circle and end up at the hotel. If there's any place else we've forgotten, we'll add it in along the way."

"Sounds like you've got it all planned out," chuckled Jack, "but if the police station is a zoo, we might have to skip it."

A few minutes later, their car slowed a bit as it pushed past the sign welcoming visitors to Valley Springs. A lone policeman sat in his patrol car, presumably looking for out-of-towners who might not have noticed the lower speed limit within the city's borders. Jack thought it was peculiar for the local police to be trolling for speeders while there were unsolved murders floating around. *Seems like his time could be better spent elsewhere,* he reasoned as he waved at the patrolman.

The patrolman returned the greeting and then slowly pulled out behind the Barnhills' Suburban. Jack glanced in his rearview mirror and reduced his speed even more. He was going under the speed limit, but one never knew with these local lawmen. Jack had worked on almost every level of law enforcement but wasn't arrogant enough to think he could talk his way out of a ticket, even in his own hometown. Heather was enthralled with the quaint little hamlet as they drove past the old library, the abandoned fire station, and the used car lot. So many memories came flooding back to her. She glanced to her right as Jack rounded the corner and eased into the bank's parking lot. Heather had worked at the bank as a youngster, and many of her coworkers were still there. They were what she referred to as "lifers"—women and men who'd grown up there, graduated high school, went to college locally, came back home to work, got married, had children, and never left. Lifers. Pillars of the community. People who rarely, if ever, ventured more than thirty miles from home, unless it was a trip to the lake or a vacation at the beach.

Jack and Heather breezed through the parking lot and into the bank lobby, where nearly everyone recognized them. There were plenty of hugs, kisses, and handshakes to go around, as word apparently leaked about their impending visit. There were no secrets—and no keeping secrets—in a small town. As the myriad bank employees and general well-wishers who had happened to enter the lobby during the mini-reception mingled about with the Barnhills, a sheriff's deputy pushed his way through the door—the same deputy who'd followed them down Main Street. All eyes darted to him as he entered, everyone there suddenly growing serious, all levity slowing to a trickle. The deputy wore a grim expression as he strode toward the couple.

"Excuse me, sir. Are you Detective Jack Barnhill?" the deputy blurted out.

"Yes, I am," Jack replied as the rest of the bank's population looked on. "How can I help you?"

"I'm Deputy Sheriff Nick Wayne of the Valley Springs Police Department. Sir, I've been sent to pick you up by my superior officer, the chief of police."

"Chief Wyatt Hart?"

"That's right, sir."

"Officer Wayne, would you happen to be Tony Wayne's son?"

"Yes, sir," Deputy Wayne replied, as emotion began to creep into his voice. He glanced down briefly to collect himself.

"I worked with your daddy. He was a good man."

"Thank you, sir."

"As a matter of fact, your chief and I both worked with your dad. I'm glad the apple didn't fall too far from the tree. You couldn't be working for a better man than Chief Hart."

"Yes, sir. I'd say he feels the same way about you. That's why he sent me down here to escort you to the station. Right away."

"He's in that big of a hurry?"

"Yes, sir. We're working a couple of major cases. I don't know if you've heard anything—"

"Just heard about it on the radio on the drive into town."

"Well, he would like your opinion and professional expertise on this," the deputy said as he glanced at his wristwatch. "I know you just got into town, but time is of the essence."

"I understand. Honey, can you handle this?"

"I suppose I could find something to do today without you," Heather smirked. "I might pick up my old shift here at the bank."

That sent all the ladies into a giggle.

"You take the keys, and I'll catch a ride back with Officer Wayne. I'll call you when I'm done. Be careful."

"You, too. I love you."

"I love you, too," Jack responded as he leaned in to kiss his wife.

The two men made their way toward the door, quickly saying their good-byes and see-you-laters to their friends. Officer Wayne's intense look returned as he climbed into the police cruiser, with Jack in tow. He cranked the car and pulled into traffic, which in Valley Springs meant a maximum of two or three cars. As they navigated the ten-minute drive to the police station, the deputy nervously tried to start a conversation with his passenger. "So, you've known Chief Hart all your life, huh?"

"I have. Ever since we were little knuckleheads in Sunday school," Jack snickered.

"When did you guys first work together?"

"At the White House, 1981."

"*The* White House?"

"Yes, sir. He's never told you?"

"No, sir."

"Okay. Let me give you the *Reader's Digest* version."

6

March 30, 1981

It was just another Monday in the life of a Secret Service agent. Special Agents Jack Barnhill and Wyatt Hart were performing their usual checks and rechecks of the immediate area surrounding the Washington Hilton Hotel in Washington DC. They still were relatively new to the detail, yet both were flourishing in their career. Their enthusiasm was contagious, so they had become an encouragement to older agents who had found the job becoming more tedious and mundane.

It had been slightly more than two months since President Ronald Reagan's inauguration, and he had already won over all of the agents with his kindness and his quick wit. They had made an oath to protect him, and out of a sense of duty to the job, they would. To know that he was the genuine article and treated them with dignity and respect instead of treating them like "the help" caused it to become even more personal to the men. It made the thought of laying down their lives for him a little more palatable.

It was nearing the end of winter, but on this day there was no sign of spring. A light mist fell from mid-morning until near the noon hour. The precipitation combined with the temperature made it seem like a cold, crisp winter day. Jack and Wyatt were quietly chatting into their earpieces as they prepared for the president's arrival.

"So is it supposed to warm up any time soon?" asked Agent Barnhill.

"I heard it was, toward the end of the week anyway," replied Agent Hart.

"Well, I wish it would. I'm gonna have to go back to Georgia soon, just to thaw out!"

"You know you love it here. You're not going back home," chided Hart good-naturedly. "This is where the action is!"

"I know, I know! You're right. I just wanna go home, eat some of Mama's home cooking, talk a little football with Dad—"

"I'll bet your dad is in hog heaven after that Sugar Bowl."

"It's been three months, and he still hasn't stopped grinning. He was so shocked and surprised and elated that *his* Georgia Bulldogs had beaten Notre Dame for the National Championship. He even wants Herschel to run for governor!"

"He'd probably win!"

Suddenly, another voice crackled into their earpieces. "Barnhill. Hart. Rawhide is saddling up Stagecoach. Get ready. We're on our way."

"We are on standby. Ten-four."

"ETA 13:50."

"Roger that."

Jack looked down at his watch. It was 1:45 p.m. The chief of security for the Secret Service was giving the agents an alert that President Reagan was in the limousine and en route to the Hilton. They made one more quick sweep of the VIP entrance to the hotel. Several members of the press were waiting, all of them properly credentialed and known to Wyatt and Jack. Right on schedule, the presidential motorcade appeared at the corner of Connecticut Avenue and T Street. The official party had arrived. Agents who were a part of the president's protection detail emerged from seemingly everywhere. Within seconds, President Reagan sprang from the car, waved to a small but growing crowd of onlookers and news media, and disappeared inside. He was there to deliver a luncheon address to representatives of the AFL-CIO, and the agents hoped it would be a quick speech. Based on how the unions felt about some of Reagan's policies, it probably would be. Most of the agents were still on high alert, but they found the time for small talk.

"How's our guy today?" Jack asked no one specifically.

"Spry and cantankerous, as always," came the reply from Agent Thomas Dell.

"You forgot stubborn," added Agent Tim Andrews. "We tried to get him to wear his bulletproof vest, and he wouldn't do it. He said it was too uncomfortable to wear. I think it's the ego—the old cowboy in him wouldn't let it happen. We kept begging him and he finally says, 'It's only a five-minute drive and a short speech to labor union reps.' I told him that he was probably right, but just in case he ticked off any of those union boys, he needed to be protected. He starts laughing and says, 'That's why I've got you guys!' We made one more run at him, but he flatly refused and wouldn't listen to any more discussion on the matter."

"All it means is that we have to focus even more on anything that seems out of the ordinary," Wyatt announced.

"Yeah, we've really gotta keep our eyes on crowd control. We're starting to get some gawkers and sightseers who are wondering why so many members of the media are present. By the old eyeball test, I'd say we're gonna have at least three hundred people or so milling around, including the press," remarked Jack.

"They've called in more DC cops to handle it," chimed in Wyatt. "They've also got a couple of plainclothes mixed in the crowd for good measure."

"The press still muttering about the Russian thing?" Tim inquired.

"That's the only reason they're here. Since he turned the Iran hostage deal around so quickly, they want to know what he's gonna do with the Soviets," Dell said.

"But what is he supposed to say? The Soviets haven't even invaded Poland ... yet."

The spirited discussion was soon interrupted by the security chief's voice in their ears. "Five minutes, guys. Focused and alert."

Jack checked his watch. 2:18 p.m.

"Wow, that was a short speech," Wyatt said.

"No change in routine," said the security chief. "We're coming back out the same way we came in. VIP corridor. T Street Northwest exit. We've got the car on the way."

Jack and the other agents began to heavily monitor the overhang area near the VIP exit. The crowd had grown so much that they had considered calling in even more law enforcement. Several policemen were acting as human barricades as the crush of onlookers surged forward. The president exited the building at almost the exact time the limousine pulled up to the curb. As he exited the hotel, the press, who were being kept back about twenty feet from the car, began to shout out their questions.

"Mr. President—"

"Mr. President, what do you plan to do about the Soviets?"

The president just smiled and waved at the onlookers, totally ignoring the media and their inquiries. The press continued with their barrage of questions.

"Have you talked with Mr. Gorbachev?"

"Do you plan on sending troops to Warsaw?"

"Mr. President! Mr. President!"

Among the shouting and camera flashbulbs popping, a man swiftly moved from the crowd of admirers. The Secret Service transmissions bounced from earpiece to earpiece, various orders being barked out from one agent to the next. In the midst of the chaotic scene, everything seemed to slow down for Agent Barnhill. He noticed the man's movement first, simply because the man was moving laterally, while everyone else was pressing forward. Jack put in a quick buzz to Agent Hart, who was standing close by.

"Wyatt, you've got a guy coming up fast. He's behind you and to your right. He's moving fast. Watch him."

"Description?"

"White male, sandy brown hair, blue coat, blue jeans," Jack spouted.

Suddenly the man cut back hard to the right and temporarily disappeared.

"Help me out, Jack. I don't see him," said Wyatt.

"Behind you and to the right. Should be moving forward, but I lost him in the crowd."

"You guys got this?" the chief of security interjected over the radio. "Get it under control quickly!"

"Look up, Wyatt! He's in front of you! Your right! Your right!" Jack screamed.

The man disappeared again.

"Dell ... Andrews ... get on it now! Help 'em out!" roared the security chief.

Agent Dell circled around from the right, while Agent Andrews doubled back and made a wide arc on the left. Seconds later, the man surfaced from the crowd again like a navy submarine.

And fired.

"Shots fired! Shots fired!" several agents screamed.

Time seemed to come to a screeching halt before Jack's brain and instincts responded. Something within his mind began to count the number of shots. *One ... two ... three ... four ... five ... six. That's all he's got,* Jack thought as he drew his service revolver. In just three short seconds, his world had spiraled into chaos and confusion. Jack raced in the direction of the president's limousine, where he saw President Reagan being shoved inside by another Secret Service agent. Jack was nearly struck by the car as it quickly sped away. Jack spun back around. Bodies were everywhere, most of them diving for cover. Several agents had pounced on a lone gunman, now lying face down on the sidewalk. Shortly after, he was subdued and carried away. The chief of security grabbed a walkie-talkie and began a mini-roll call of his agents.

"All agents! What've we got? Anyone down?"

"Agent Dell, sir! Argghh! I---I think I took a shot in the back! I need some help here!"

Help was on the way, as the rest of the agents instantly checked in with the chief.

"Anyone heard from Andrews?"

"Sir, he just went by me on a stretcher. Looks like he got shot in the gut," said a clearly concerned Agent Hart.

"Okay, here's the situation. The gunman squeezed off six shots. He hit four people: Agent Dell, Agent Andrews, the president's press secretary Jim Brady, and unfortunately, Rawhide himself. Mr. Brady's in bad shape.

The president is alive but is on his way to George Washington Hospital. That's it so far. Let's take a couple of minutes to gather ourselves and then get to work. We need witnesses and statements. We've got a job to do. Let's not drop the ball again on this one."

$$\Omega$$

Over the next week to ten days, President Reagan would continue to recover, as well as Agents Dell and Andrews, who were able to resume their jobs after a successful rehabilitation period. Press Secretary Jim Brady was not as lucky. He sustained a serious head injury and would later become permanently disabled.

Six weeks later, the repercussions of the assassination attempt caught up with the agents, who were a part of the president's protection team. Very quickly and very quietly, so as not to draw the attention of the media, several agents were reassigned to different details. Many of them felt that they were unfairly singled out, scapegoats to a major security snafu by the security chief, who would offer no defense for them. Among those who were reassigned and disillusioned by their new detail were Agents Jack Barnhill and Wyatt Hart, who were shuttled out to Plains, Georgia, to become part of former President Jimmy Carter's team. A few months later, both agents would tender their resignations, citing burnout as the reason. However, they would not be out of work for very long.

Ω 7

"Well, dang. Can't a man drive through a town to look for his retirement home without being pulled over by the local yokels?" Jack chided as he walked through the door leading to the forensics lab. Chief Wyatt Hart immediately knew that voice without turning around.

"If you hadn't been breaking the land-speed record coming into town, I wouldn't have to!" Chief Hart joked. He pushed himself up from the stool where he was seated and gave Jack the typical male greeting: handshake, brief hug, and three quick slaps on the back. "It's been a long time, Jack. Great to see ya."

"So much for sneaking into town, huh?"

"You oughta know that you can't keep any secrets in a small town, so I figured I'd just send for you. Saves us both time!" Despite his jovial dialogue, Chief Hart looked horrible, as if he hadn't slept in days. In reality, it was nearing the twenty-hour mark since he *had* slept. His clothes and hair were quite disheveled, and his cheeks and chin had sprouted a coat of stubble. He'd been in the "dungeon," as the other policemen liked to call the forensics lab, for nearly the whole twenty hours, even though the main entrance to the station house was only a few yards down the small corridor. All the facilities, including the interrogation room, the holding cells, the reception area, and even the morgue, were contained in this one building. It was convenient most of the time, but now, it was threatening to become a problem, especially with both of the open cases he was working.

"Wow, I know you're ugly, but this is over the top! When's the last time you took a break?" kidded Jack.

"It's easier to stay down here. Two open murder cases. People in town are already starting to panic. I'd just as soon hole up in here, so I don't have to answer all their questions right now. I wouldn't know what to tell them. The worst part is that at any minute, you know the press is gonna be breathing down my neck."

"Wyatt, I know how you are, but you've got to take a break. Take a step back before this all becomes … claustrophobic to you."

"Sorta why I had you 'arrested.' Rumor had it you were coming into town, so I needed a fresh pair of eyes to help sort this thing out. A little professional courtesy, so to speak. For old times' sake."

"You know, I'm glad you asked. I was gonna purposely stay away when I heard about your situation. Funny thing was, I didn't want it to seem like I was trying to 'big city' you. At the same time, I would have been disappointed if I had come back into town for the week and didn't get to hang out with you."

"Never thought it would be under these conditions, huh?"

"Nope."

"First murders we've had in Valley Springs since the 1930s," Hart stated matter-of-factly.

"Okay, that's it. Call Mama K's and order two plates to go. We'll eat a late lunch. That'll give you a break. Then you can brief me on what you've got."

"I'm not really that—"

"You need to eat, Wyatt. We'll look at everything after we eat. I'll sleep on it. *You'll* sleep on it. Then we'll go from there. Right now, all you need to know is this: fried chicken, black-eyed peas, mashed potatoes with gravy, cornbread, and sweet tea."

Wyatt shook his head and laughed. His friend always had the ability to cut to the chase and to diffuse any difficult or tense situation by means of humor, hunger, or any other possible way. "Some things never change," Wyatt cracked. The irony of his statement settled over him like a blanket. Indeed, most things in a small town never did change. Now, suddenly, they had. The way in which he responded to this change in normalcy would determine if the town would ever be the same.

Ω

Deputy Wayne didn't mind playing the role of delivery boy, as he rapped on the door of the forensics lab holding a bag of fresh country home-cooking. Jack and Wyatt took the plates and hid in a small office in the corner of the lab. Wyatt had briefed Jack on who was in the know about the cases. He'd managed to keep it to a select few: the medical examiner, Dr. London Brown, and his assistant; Deputy Wayne; two other night-shift officers; and the dispatcher. He fanned out all the paperwork, any leads he had scribbled down, and any other clues he'd managed to piece together. However, Jack wouldn't let him go through any of it until they'd eaten.

"Let's bless this, so we can eat and get back to the cases," Hart said urgently.

"Okay. Relax, Wyatt. We're gonna get this guy but not on an empty stomach. I'll pray. I've got a feeling your prayer would be 'Good food. Good meat. Good Lord, let's eat!'"

Wyatt finally burst into a hearty laugh, the kind he hadn't had in quite a few days. He bowed his head as Jack began to pray.

"Lord, we thank You for this day. We thank You for all the blessings that You give us. I pray for my brother Wyatt, Lord, and ask that you give him clarity of mind and purity of thought as he solves these two cases. May You alone be glorified as he brings this criminal to justice. Now, bless this food to the nourishment of our bodies, so that we can serve You with all of our strength. We love You, Lord, and it's in Your name that we pray. Amen."

The two men dug in to their carry-out orders, Jack with the fried chicken and Wyatt with the cubed steak, fried okra, and whole kernel corn. They chit-chatted about all of the happenings in Valley Springs. All the old men still had coffee at Mama K's early in the morning and then went to Spicer's Pharmacy until lunchtime. Spicer's had an old-fashioned soda fountain in the back of the store that didn't work anymore, but it was a nostalgic place for all of the old-timers to congregate. Doc Morgan was nearing his seventies, but he continued to man the pharmacy counter. Spicer's still made home deliveries and continued the practice of letting customers run up a tab. The women around town kept the beauty parlors abuzz with the most recent and juiciest bits of gossip. The same people that Jack had known for years were working in the same places at the three grocery stores, the two florists, the two hardware stores, the radio station, and the library. This town was a living, breathing time capsule.

Slowly, Jack and Wyatt's conversation meandered back toward the two cases. As they finished up the last tasty morsels, Chief Hart began to lay out all the evidence, paperwork, 9-1-1 tapes, and any other pieces of information they'd picked up along the way. He scooped up and discarded the two empty Styrofoam trays, took a deep breath, and painted the picture for Jack.

"Okay, here goes. The first death occurred two weeks ago on a Saturday night. Young female hung by her ankles from the old fire tower. She had been out drinking and someone apparently drugged her. Tox screen showed two benzodiazepines in her system. She had a prescription for the first one but not for the second one. The second one is much stronger. That's what he used to knock her out. We also found significant levels of epinephrine in her system."

"You think the alcohol had anything to do with it?" Jack interjected.

"Dr. Brown doesn't think so. He checked her chart, and she was diagnosed eighteen months ago with acrophobia, which is why she had the benzo in her system."

"Fear of heights, huh?"

"Yep, which makes me think our perp knew her medical history. Why else would he knock her out, just to wake her up again by shooting her full of epinephrine?"

"If he wanted to kill her, why didn't he go ahead and drop her from the tower?"

"Exactly. It's like he's trying to make a point. That's what I think the inscription on the index card means."

Jack picked up the clear plastic bag containing the index card. He held it up to the light, examining it for any sign of a clue. "No fingerprints on the card? Swept clean?"

"You got it."

"Hmm … 'Face Your Fears.' What is that?" Jack said as he paced the floor.

"I don't know. I mean, it kinda sounds like a call to be brave. Some kind of mantra he's using. The thing I don't get is the red omega symbol. I've been wracking my brain, and I don't see what one has to do with the other."

"So, what about the second case?" asked Jack.

"Happened a week ago in an abandoned farmhouse out past County Road 35," said Wyatt as he unfurled a map of the county and circled the approximate location with his pen. "Another anxiety-related heart failure. A housewife was duct taped to a chair and basically buried alive by spiders."

Jack froze in his tracks, then turned and pointed at Wyatt, a knowing look on his face.

"Let me guess … arachnophobia."

"Bingo. Same MO. Benzos and epinephrine."

"What kind of spiders did he use?"

"What *kind*?"

"Yeah, black widows, brown widows, brown recluses?"

"I'm not sure. Let me pull one out of evidence."

Wyatt dug through a small cardboard box until he found the plastic specimen jar. The insect inside was not alive but was intact and had been carefully preserved at the crime scene. He set it gently on the table in front of Jack.

Immediately, Jack's eyes lit up. "Wyatt, you've got a thinker on your hands. A cerebral type."

"What do you mean?"

"You were right. He's using their own personal fears against them. It's not the objects he's using, per se; it's the final result. He's not actively killing them. He's basically letting them kill themselves."

"Okay, but what does that have to do with our spider friend here?"

"That's not a spider."

Ω 8

"I'm sorry. What am I missing here?" quizzed Chief Hart.

"I knew those entomology classes at the academy would pay off eventually," Jack said. "That technically is *not* a spider."

"Technically?"

"Well, look at its body. Normally, a spider's body has two parts: the cephalothorax and the abdomen. This 'spider' has its head, thorax, and abdomen all fused together in one piece. Therefore, it's not a spider."

"Jack, that's a spider! It has eight legs. Those things are found everywhere around here. We used to call them daddy longlegs when we were kids."

"Let me get all scientific on you for just a minute. The term that entomologists use for a daddy longlegs is 'harvestman.' The harvestman is more closely related to ticks and mites than it is to spiders, even though it has eight legs and looks like a spider. Here's the take-home point: they are nonthreatening! They don't even bite. They are nonpoisonous."

"Really?"

"There's no need to fear them because they contain no venom at all. None!"

"Well, thank you, Mr. Know-It-All."

"I do what I can."

"So that just proves our point—that this guy knows what he's doing. The average Joe wouldn't have known that these harvestmen couldn't hurt a fly. Heck, *I* didn't even know."

"Now imagine an average Joe with arachnophobia."

That brought a somber, thoughtful silence between them. Wyatt breathed a long sigh and stated the obvious. "Scares them to death. Almost brilliant if it weren't so sick and twisted."

Just then, Jack's cell phone began to vibrate in his shirt pocket. He checked the caller ID. Heather. He held up a finger to Wyatt and clicked the talk button. "Hi, honey. How's it going?"

"Great. Getting reacquainted with half of the population of Valley Springs. How's it going with you?"

"Good. Going through some casework with Wyatt. What's up?"

"Well, everyone's asking when you'll be coming by. They're all dying to see you too." Heather quickly shifted the tone of her conversation to get to the real reason why she'd called Jack. "I finally ran into Annette at the florist, and she wants us to go to dinner with them tonight. Annette and Wyatt. You and me. That's it."

"Uh, I'm—"

"Annette insists that we go with them. She wants you to make Wyatt get out of the station for a few hours. I know you guys are working hard on the cases, but you need to take a break. *Wyatt* needs to take a break."

Jack was between a rock and a hard place. On one hand, he knew the ladies were right. Wyatt needed a respite from the office and a few hours of sleep. On the other hand, he knew that the suggestion would fall on deaf ears with Wyatt. Jack didn't want to be the one to tell Wyatt to get out of his own police station and blow off some steam. Jack was only a visitor here now, and he felt that it wasn't his place to say. Besides, they'd just eaten and were still full.

"Well, I—"

"I'm going over to the hotel to freshen up," Heather interrupted him again. She was excited to see her friend again, and Jack could tell that she really wanted to go. In fact, she insisted on going. "It'll take me about an hour or so. Annette's picking me up there around six o'clock, and then we're coming by to get you guys. Hope Marinara's is okay with you."

"That's fine. I'll see what I can do."

"Love you. See you at six."

"Love you, too. Bye." He clicked off the cell phone and blew out a long breath.

Wyatt had known Jack long enough to know what that meant. "What are we getting roped into now?" he inquired.

"Dinner with the wives. Six o'clock. Marinara's."

"Figures. I need to get out of here anyway. I'm nearly cross-eyed looking at all this stuff."

"You need some sleep."

"I know, I know."

The two men gathered up all their case materials, locked them in Chief Hart's office, and strolled into the small courtyard adjacent to the police station. They rehashed a few more minor details about the cases before their conversation began to veer in a different direction. Next thing they knew, Annette's sedan was pulling up to the curb with their waving and giggling wives inside.

"Is it six already?" asked Jack.

"Apparently so," replied Wyatt, somewhat sheepishly.

"All right, you two," Annette shouted as she rolled down her window. "Let's go! We're starving!"

"Do you always pick up your men this way?"

"Only the good-looking ones. The rest we kidnap and keep in the trunk," Heather snickered.

$$\Omega$$

The dinner was wonderful, the conversation rollicking, and the company second to none. The clock edged its way toward nine o'clock as the evening wound to a close. After they exchanged cars and good-night embraces, the Barnhills steered the Suburban through their old hometown and into the parking lot of the hotel, located just a few miles away. Heather had already had their luggage brought up to the room, much to her husband's delight. It had been a long, exciting day for the Barnhills, but now they were exhausted and ready for bed. Heather handed off the keycard to Jack as they exited the elevator and slogged down the hall toward the room. He slid the card into the slot upside down, making the red light wink.

Still locked. He flipped the card over and tried again. A click and a green light. As he pushed the door open, his eyes were diverted toward the carpeted floor. Something was directly ahead, immediately capturing his attention. Jack's tired, bleary eyes darted to the left, just past the shadow of the doorframe. On the floor lay what appeared to be a business card, only slightly larger in size, yet similar to what a salesman might give a potential customer. Jack instinctively threw up his arm to keep Heather back. She stood motionless in the doorway, following his eyes to the small card lying on the carpet. He could only make out a small part of the message on the card without picking it up, but he knew the message was meant for him.

"Wait here," he instructed Heather.

He cautiously pushed the door completely open and stepped into the bathroom. Grabbing the plastic ice bucket liner and the bucket's top, Jack dropped to his knees and crawled over to the index card. Heather watched in wide-eyed amazement and curiosity as he scooped up the card without using his hands and deposited it into the clear plastic bag. "Okay, come in and close the door!"

Heather dashed in and double-locked the door, suddenly alarmed by Jack's urgent tone of voice. A gnawing fear rose within her. She couldn't take her eyes away from the bag, now dangling from her husband's fingertips. He held it high, twisting it back and forth, bringing it right in front of his face and then held it back up to the light, looking for any sign or clue of its origin. After what seemed like days, she broke the silence that hung ominously over the room. "Jack, what's going on? What is that?"

"Looks like it could be a potential problem," he muttered after a few more seconds of deliberation.

"What do you mean a 'problem'? For us?"

"A component of the two cases that Wyatt is working on involves a calling card of sorts. An index card with some words, some phrases, and some symbols written on it."

"And this is one of those cards?" she asked.

"Yep."

"How did it get here? Better yet, how did anyone know we were staying in this room?"

"I guess someone heard we were coming to town. Secrets don't last very long in a place like Valley Springs."

"So this guy obviously knows us and knows where we're staying. My God, Jack! This killer ... this monster ... knows us, which means we probably know him!"

Jack countered with a few seconds of silence before he meekly offered up a response. "Probably."

"We've gotta call Wyatt."

"No, not yet. He's worn to a frazzle. I don't wanna dump this on him tonight. Let him get some sleep. I've got the card bagged up as evidence. After he gets some rest, I'll give it to him first thing. With his workaholic personality, he'll probably wake *me* up in the morning."

Heather didn't really like his answer, but she knew he was right. Still, her curiosity got the best of her. "So what does it say on the card?" Jack hesitated, trying to stall for time, but Heather had seen this reaction before. When Jack hemmed and hawed, she snapped, "Would you just tell me? I appreciate you trying to protect me, but I can handle it. And if it's related to the case, I can keep a secret, too. I know you're surprised, but I really can!"

Usually, Jack would find the humor in her sarcasm, but today was not the day. This was too serious. This was too personal.

"Read it," she urged once again.

He sighed. The words gave him chills every time he read them. "It says 'Jack and Heather. Still together ... but not forever. Face your fears.'"

Conspicuously in the center of the card loomed a red symbol. The last letter of the Greek alphabet: omega.

9

Jack and Heather spent a mostly sleepless night, tossing and turning. They were creatures of habit and probably wouldn't have had a good night's rest simply because they weren't in their own bed. Now, though, the realization that the Barnhills more than likely knew the killer and the killer also knew them really set Jack and Heather on edge. Before they'd attempted to go to sleep, Jack dashed back out to the Suburban and retrieved his service revolver, just in case. Emergencies occasionally popped up, and this was one of those instances. His mind had been racing all night, trying to remember every single person in Valley Springs who might have had it in for him or Heather. The majority of people were nice folks, most of them not even close to being suspects. The sad thing was that in cases like this, *everyone* was a suspect. The trick was to eliminate suspects, which was a slow, grueling process of sorting out alibis and corroborating eyewitness accounts. All of the thoughts crossing his mind were suddenly flushed away when his cell phone began to chirp. He swiftly rolled over and glanced at the clock. 6:30 a.m. Grabbing the phone, he checked the caller ID before answering. It was Wyatt.

"Hello?" Jack sleepily answered.

"Morning, Jack," said Wyatt. "Sorry to wake you."

"It's okay. I didn't sleep that well anyway. How about you? Did you get some rest?" he said as he rubbed his eyes.

"I slept a little. I needed the rest, but my mind's been in overdrive. Why didn't you sleep? Bed too uncomfortable?"

"No, not really. We got back to the hotel, and when we opened our door … well, let's just say we became a part of your case."

"I'm sorry; I don't follow you."

"When we got to the room we found that someone had left us a calling card on the floor. A slightly oversized business card or a smaller sized index card," Jack said as he braced for his friend's reaction.

"An index card!" Chief Hart exclaimed. "What does it say? And why didn't you call me?"

"Because it was late, and I knew you needed some sleep. I've got it bagged for your evidence guys," he said as he rolled onto his side.

"What did the card say? Did he threaten you?"

"Sorta. He made a veiled threat, but—"

"All right, get dressed," Wyatt interrupted him. "I'll be over to get you in half an hour."

"I'm not leaving Heather by herself."

"I'll get Annette to come over and wait with Heather. I'll also put someone on the door. Twenty-four-hour security for as long as you're here," Wyatt said, his voice rising. "If the girls want to go somewhere, the security team goes with them."

"But aren't your guys already stretched pretty thin?" he agonized as he ran a hand over his face.

"Look, I'll be honest with you, Jack. I need your help on this one. If you're having to worry about your safety or Heather's safety, your mind won't be where it ought to be. It's not where I *need* it to be. Now, that's that! I'm getting in my car now. I'll be there in thirty minutes. Be ready."

"OK. I'll see you in thirty."

Heather had heard most of Jack's side of the conversation in the stillness of the early morning. It was Saturday, the day most people tended to sleep in a little longer than normal. This day was anything but normal, and she'd gotten very little sleep. Jack rolled out of bed and headed for the bathroom. He sighed loudly, partly from fatigue, partly from worry. Heather pushed herself up and whispered to him, "So where are you gonna stash Annette and me today?"

"Nowhere if you don't want to be."

"Are you kidding me? It gives me just another excuse to hang out with

Annette! It sounded as if Wyatt will have some kind of security with us, so I'm not too nervous about it. Besides, you and Wyatt have a lot of evidence to cover. I want this creep off the streets. He's messing with the wonderful memories I have of my hometown—our hometown. He's turning it from an image of a Norman Rockwell painting to an image of Norman Bates!"

Jack had to chuckle at the reference. How she could have a sense of humor about such a serious situation was beyond him. He felt a little better about leaving her but not *much* better.

$$\Omega$$

Thirty minutes later, the two men were back at it, reviewing old evidence and inspecting the new index card. Once again, they had no new leads. The card was ordinary and swept completely clean of fingerprints. The only thing they could concentrate on at this point was the motive. The cards left at the other murder scenes had said the same thing, but this one singled out Jack and Heather, who were still very much alive. Why? This was the puzzle they worked on until late Saturday night. In the meantime, Annette and Heather had gone to the Harts' home, where they prepared the guest room for the Barnhills. After Heather told Annette the story about the index card in their hotel room, Annette had insisted that they check out immediately and spend the rest of the week with them. There was safety in numbers, she'd reasoned, and two couples plus an extra security person was about as safe as one could possibly expect to be. Midway through that same afternoon, they'd called the guys to check up on them and let them know about the new housing arrangements. They'd also coerced the men into a promise to be home by seven that night. A quick spaghetti dinner and an early bedtime were in order for tonight. Tomorrow was Sunday, and they all needed as much time with the Lord as they could get. It had been a long forty-eight hours.

$$\Omega$$

"And I know how hard these last couple of weeks have been on you. I feel the same way, too." Jack's mind was gradually drifting back to the sermon. It wasn't that Pastor Noel Marshall's sermons were boring. In fact, quite the opposite was true. For such a small town, Pastor Marshall seemed out of place, as if he belonged at a large suburban mega-church. He preached with fire, fervency, and an urgency that even startled his own congregation at times. This was the only place in town where *laid-back* was not the operative word. He'd had his offers to go elsewhere, but this was his home, until the Lord told him to pull up stakes. Jack thought that the pastor of his home church in Atlanta was the absolute best, but Pastor Marshall was a close second. He forced his brain to refocus on the pastor and pushed the unsolved cases temporarily out of his mind.

"But this is what we need to remember. We can be concerned. We *should* be concerned. That's just our nature. It's the way God made us. If we *truly* trust in God, like we say we do, then we have no room in our lives for worry, we have no room in our lives for anxiety, and we have *no* room in our lives for fear! In fact, I'll take it a step farther. When we have worries, anxieties, and fears that creep into our consciousness and crowd out our faith in Him, we are temporarily acting as atheists. Our tiny little brains won't believe that God can handle it, so we try to do it in our own strength. That's a strong statement on what we *say* and what we *believe*. Look into your own heart. Do you totally trust Him? Have faith in Him? Or when times get tough, are you a temporary atheist? Let's see what God's Word says about fear. The Bible says in several places that the fear of the Lord is the beginning of wisdom. Proverbs 8:13 takes it up a notch from wisdom by saying that to fear the Lord is to hate evil. Flip over a page or two to Proverbs 10:27, where it says that the fear of the Lord prolongs life. In that same vein, Proverbs 14:27 states that the fear of the Lord is a fountain of life that turns people from the snares of death. I don't know about you, but I'm sold! The only thing I want to fear is the Lord! Why? Let me count the ways. First of all, we're commanded to do so. Second, it leads to wisdom. Is there anyone out there who doesn't want to be smarter or wiser?"

That remark drew nervous chuckles from almost everyone in the congregation. The pastor continued his point. "The third reason we should fear the Lord is because it confirms our hatred of evil, and this person's … actions, committing the heinous crimes, are definitely evil. The fourth point is the knowledge that the fear of the Lord also prolongs life, and the final point is that the fear of the Lord can turn people away from death. Each one of these is reason enough, but all of these are *more than* reason enough. I don't know about you, but I never, ever want to be remembered for my lack of faith or my lack of trust in Him! I will not be a temporary atheist because of what this beast has chosen to do!"

A smattering of applause and a few scattered amens drifted toward the pulpit. At that moment, Deputy Nick Wayne stuck his head through the door in the back of the church. He peered around the congregation, drawing curious stares from the parishioners, including Pastor Marshall. Both Jack and Wyatt swiveled their heads toward the rear door once they'd noticed the tiny commotion Deputy Wayne was causing. Ultimately catching their eyes, the deputy made a motion with his hand, signaling both of them to meet him in the vestibule that led to the exit. The look on the deputy's face told them everything they needed to know. There was another victim.

Victim number three.

10

She awoke to what felt like sandpaper sliding across her face. Wet sandpaper. Her drug-induced stupor didn't allow her eyes to focus on exactly what was passing over her right cheek. Whatever it was, the young woman knew it was out of the ordinary. As she gradually gathered her wits about her and desperately tried to shake the buzzing from her head, it was only then that she realized exactly where she was. Casting her eyes toward the ceiling, she felt another piece of the wet sandpaper skidding over her chin and neck. This was the inside of her home, the master bathroom to be more precise. And if she wasn't mistaken, she was lying in her hot tub. A hot tub with no water in it. Her hands were positioned over her head, but she couldn't move them. The duct tape yanked them even higher as the handcuffs sliced into both wrists. She struggled to break free of the restraints that had been attached to the tub's downspout. Now her back was starting to cramp and ache from fatigue, and in trying to gain relief from the pain, she discovered that someone had placed her in a head-and-neck restraint.

Sssssst!

The woman saw a long, thin pink tongue shoot directly across the middle of her right eye.

What was that? She caught a flash of green out of the corner of her eye. A yellowish-ivory object slid past her field of vision. Now she recognized exactly what it was and suddenly began to panic. She struggled against the restraints, glancing down toward her toes. But her toes were nowhere to be found. Instead, all she could see was a huge tangle of thin, green, slithering snakes draped around her legs. *Snakes!* The young woman's heart pounded inside her chest so loudly that she could practically hear it. Her breathing became labored, as if she was being smothered by a blanket. In her mind, she *was* being smothered. Almost immediately, her body broke into a cold sweat, and goose bumps covered every inch of her skin. She had to get up! She had to get out! Her eyes appeared to bulge out of their sockets as she tried to push herself up by using her feet, but it was no use. Looking down only made things worse. The snakes had begun to entwine themselves around nearly the length of her body, from armpits to toenails. They weren't squeezing and they weren't biting, but it didn't matter. Her body and mind were already in a full-blown meltdown. Her fists went from open to clenched, open to clenched. The tone of her skin morphed from natural to crimson to white. Her wrists were growing even more red and raw from attempting to escape the handcuffs. A small trickle of blood seeped out from underneath the duct tape. Every vein, every artery appeared to be on the edge of explosion. Her muscles were tightening and starting to cramp again. She finally mustered the energy to let out a throat-ripping scream.

"Eeeeeee!"

Then the screams wouldn't stop coming.

"Eeeeeee! Eeeeeee! Eeeeeee!"

The screaming just made the snakes wiggle around faster, which made her screech longer and louder. This vicious circle continued for what seemed like hours but was actually just a few minutes. The only thing that stopped her shrieking was a thin, slithering tail that accidently dropped onto her tongue. She quickly spit it out, but the image of the snake's tail sliding across her lips set off a new round of screams. It was only then, in the semi-darkness of the room, that the girl noticed shadows rippling across the ceiling. Was it her shadow? The snakes? No! Someone else was in the house with her. Watching her. Help. Help had arrived! Or had it? Was this her savior? Or her captor? It didn't matter. All her brain could think to do was scream.

"Help! Help me! Please!" She couldn't see him because of the restraints, but she knew he was there. She could sense his presence.

A slight chuckle eased its way from his throat as he dialed the phone number.

"9-1-1. What is your emergency, please?"

"Um … yes. I'd like to report a case of a reptile dysfunction."

"I'm sorry?"

Just then, the girl let loose with another series of horrifying shrieks.

"Sir, is everything all right?" the operator questioned.

"Well, duh! No, that's kinda why I called, remember?"

"Talk to me, sir. What's happening?"

"Help me! Help me, please!" the girl screamed.

"Hold on just one second," the man interjected.

The operator could hear the girl's screams become muffled.

The man had shoved a washcloth into her mouth. When he returned to the phone, he said in mock frustration, "There. Don't you absolutely hate it when people interrupt you?"

"Sir, is the woman okay?"

"*Ma'am!* Didn't we already have this conversation? You know, with today being Sunday and all, ya gotta figure there's some real weirdos out there. And believe me, I know weird. Snake handlers and such. It's an abomination, I tell ya."

"Sir, are you okay?"

The man ignored the question and continued his rambling train of thought. "Church folks not acting like church folks should, I mean. This town is full of hypocrites! This town used to be on fire for Jesus. Now, I'd just love to see it burn. Valley Springs isn't the lighthouse it used to be. It's a snake pit. Which brings me back to my dear friend here. Let's call her Eve, since the 'serpents' are all around her. She's literally swimming in a hot tub full of snakes and believe me, I know how she feels! Isn't that just so symbolic?"

"I'm sorry?"

"I've got a young lady here who loves her hot tub, but not *snakes* in her hot tub. Go figure."

"Sir, we need to send help. Can you tell me the address?"

"I could, but that wouldn't be much fun now, would it? I'll tell you what. I'm gonna make my way out of here, but I'll give you a teeny hint. The street name you're looking for is the same color as these snakes. Now let's see how *sssss*smart you are, my darling."

"Can you give—"

"And by the way, you might want to *sssss*send animal control too. Ta-ta for now. Happy hunting!!"

The operator had attempted to trace the call while she had him on the line, but to no avail. The caller was somehow able to scramble his phone number and his call's point of origin, so she was unable to pinpoint him or his location. Left to her own devices, the operator knew that there were only two streets in Valley Springs with colors in their name: Orange Street and Green Street. She hastily deduced that it probably wasn't Orange Street because the majority of people who lived there were elderly, and the screams sounded as if they were from someone much younger. Besides, the caller said that the street's name was the same color as the snakes. Snakes would more often be green than orange. It had to be Green Street. She hurriedly pulled up the grid of addresses along Green Street. Scanning the occupants, she came across the phone listings of two women who were listed as head of household. The first lived at 3226 Green Street. Doris Browning, age fifty-six. Perhaps a little too old for the kind of screams she'd heard over her earpiece. The operator scrolled down to the next one on the computer screen. Natalie Watson, age twenty-four. It had to be her. Going on pure instinct, she radioed to the policemen who were out on patrol.

"Valley Springs dispatch radioing all available cars. Possible 187 at 3410 Green Street. Suspect may still be on or near the premises. Use extreme caution."

"Is it him?" one of the patrolmen squawked over the air.

"Sounds like him. Be careful, guys."

In less than two minutes, three squad cars screeched to a halt in front of Natalie Watson's modest one-story home. When no one answered after the first knock, a police officer kicked in the front door. With guns drawn, the officers slowly made their way through the home. As they approached the bathroom, the officer on point pulled up short, nearly causing the others behind him to crash into him. A gigantic tangle of green snakes were writhing around a figure that appeared only to be a set of arms and legs.

The point officer spoke into his radio. "Attention, dispatch. I think we've got another one. I can't tell for sure if she's dead or alive. She's in a Jacuzzi, covered by approximately one hundred to one hundred fifty green snakes. They're wiggling all over the place, so we can't determine if it's her breathing or if it's the snakes. We're gonna need animal control down here so we can have somewhere to put these babies. Right now, they're contained in the tub, but we've gotta get to the body."

"Ten-four. Copy that. Help is on the way."

"Oh, and somebody better get Chief Hart out of church. He's not gonna like this."

11

It was early Monday morning, but the sleepy little town of Valley Springs was not very quiet on this particular day. Media trucks from the Southeast and all over the nation were setting up shop, intrigued by the story that had leaked from this Mayberry-like town. The sounds of churning generators provided enough noise to give the roosters a well-earned and much-deserved day off. Engineers were scurrying about, putting up lights for the live shots. Reporters were popping in and out of the news vans, touching up their hair and checking their makeup. Satellites were tilted and adjusted until the feed was perfect. Now all that was left to do was watch the clock. It was approaching the top of the hour, and the race was on. Some of the townspeople had awakened early and flipped on their televisions, only to find out that *they* were the news.

$$\Omega$$

"I'm Amanda Sutter, reporting live from the little town of Valley Springs, Georgia, where a manhunt is on for the person or persons responsible for the deaths of at least three young women over the past three weeks. It's been decades since this small hamlet has had a homicide within its city limits. In fact, it's been over seventy years since a murder has been recorded here in Valley Springs. You can imagine what three murders in three weeks can do to the psyche of its residents and local law enforcement."

They cut to a taped segment shot just minutes ago at Mama K's, as a few of the old timers gave their opinions on the latest developments. Some were afraid. Others were defiant. A couple blamed the police for not doing anything to stop it. Most of them wished that the whole thing, media and all, would just go away and leave them to their isolation once again. The segment wound down and the camera went back to the live feed.

"All three victims are females in their mid-twenties to mid-thirties. Sources have revealed to us that the women were apparently drugged and then left to die, not murdered gruesomely, as was previously reported erroneously. However, the killer supposedly leaves a note with each victim, reportedly a small index card, with a red omega symbol in the center, the meaning of which is unclear. He has been dubbed the Omega Killer by some media outlets, but very little else is known about him. Investigators are being extremely tight-lipped about what their next move might be, but word may be coming down this afternoon. I'm Amanda Sutter. Now back to you guys in the studio."

$$\Omega$$

The police station was in a virtual lockdown. No one got in unless they were invited, and no one left unless they were crazy. The media were camped outside, eager to pounce on anyone who exited the building. Deep in the recesses of the police complex, four men and one woman were seated around a conference room table, waiting for a sixth member of their team to arrive. Wyatt and Jack leaned over the table, studying new evidence from the most recent case. The medical examiner, Dr. London Brown, held a manila folder in his lap and read over his lab finding. Special Agent-in-Charge Martin Spikes of the Georgia Bureau of Investigation was making mental notes on each case, taking bits from the conversation between Wyatt and Jack, as well as his own comparisons with the forensic scientist/psychologist he'd brought along with him. Dr. Alexis Sheffield had been with the Bureau for nearly twelve months, yet in that short amount of time she'd established herself as one of its most valuable members, based on the number of cases solved utilizing evidence that she'd collected. The sixth man was an unknown commodity, but he was an agent from the FBI, coming at the request of the GBI. The chattering continued for another five minutes before the receptionist buzzed into the conference room.

"Chief Hart, a Hardin Duvall is here from the FBI."

The announcement of his name sent shivers through Wyatt's spine, but he held it together long enough to muster up a response. "Send him in."

Jack and Wyatt locked eyes. Each one knew what the other was thinking. Their minds raced back to 1981. The chief of security for President Reagan at the time of John Hinckley's assassination attempt. The one who'd made a scapegoat out of several Secret Service agents when, in fact, it had been his own negligence that had led to the shooting. His name? Hayden Duvall. Could it be his brother?

"Hardin Duvall, FBI," he said, extending his hand to Wyatt first, then to Jack, Dr. Brown, Agent Spikes, and Dr. Sheffield. "Nice to meet you. Wish it was under different circumstances."

One look at the man and they both knew. Jack and Wyatt never imagined that the man who had altered both of their careers in the early 1980s had a twin brother. As the group exchanged pleasantries, Jack felt a wave of heat spread up his spine. *Of all the people they could've sent from the Bureau, why did they have to pick* this *guy?* he thought. Each one swiftly took a seat around the conference room table, with Duvall taking his place at the head chair. He wasted no time in getting to the heart of the matter.

"Just a little housekeeping here, and then we're gonna jump in with both feet. Officer Barnhill, we understand that you are here on vacation and working under the auspices of Chief Hart, since you are technically out of your jurisdiction. Is that correct, Chief Hart?"

"Yes, sir, it is," responded Wyatt.

"I don't have a problem with any extra help, but make sure that the chain of command stays intact. We also understand that you received a little 'love note' from our perpetrator, so in order to keep it from being a conflict of interest with you working this case, it's gotta be under Chief Hart's command. Is that clear?"

"I understand," said Jack.

"Good. We've already contacted your superiors at Atlanta PD, and they said you are okayed to stay here as long as is necessary. After your vacation week is up, they'll move your status to paid leave of absence, with department permission. You and your wife all right with housing?"

"Yes, sir."

"Super. Glad to have you on board. Everyone else set up with housing, transportation, et cetera?"

The group nodded as a whole.

"Anything else you can think of before we dive in?"

No one moved or spoke.

"All right, let's start with the local guys and work our way up. You all know most of the details of each case. If you need to refer back to them, they're in the files in front of you. Can one of you Valley Springs guys give me the who, what, where, when, and why of the cases and any thoughts, feelings, leanings, or suspicions on this guy?"

All eyes skipped toward Chief Hart, who nervously cleared his throat. "Well, I guess I'll start. We're pretty certain that he's a local guy, based on the fact that he knew Detective Barnhill and his wife, both of whom grew up here. He's smart, possibly with a medical background—"

"What makes you say that?" Duvall queried.

"Because he has access to patient medical histories. He's carefully choosing patients who've been diagnosed with specific anxiety disorders. The first victim had acrophobia. The second had arachnophobia. The most recent one, ophidiophobia."

"Ophidiophobia?"

"Fear of snakes."

"But does that mean he has medical experience just because he knows a little about anxiety disorders?"

"No, but he knows which medications knock them out, suppress their memories, and wake them up in time for their own death. He also has access to these particular drugs right now, in real time."

"Let's look at his personality a little bit closer. Dr. Brown or Dr. Sheffield, what are your impressions of this guy, clinically speaking?"

Dr. Sheffield held out her hand first, in deference to Dr. Brown.

"If I may speak candidly," Dr. Brown began, "I think his methods are carefully orchestrated. He's a little crazy, but he has a sense of humor, so he's not *totally* nuts. Above all, he's very clever, almost brilliant in that he leaves no traces of himself. He knows what he's doing. He's not actively killing his victims, but he sets it up so that the victims, through their anxiety disorder, basically kill themselves. It's the easiest way for him to kill others. He doesn't have to get his hands dirty."

"So let's talk about these anxiety disorders, these … phobias. Dr. Sheffield?"

"Well, phobias are intense fears that can trigger an anxiety-type response. That response could be in the form of specific symptoms, such as a pounding or racing heart rate, a feeling of smothering or choking, chest pain, sweating, dizziness, trembling, nausea, chills, or hot flashes. The most telling symptom we see is an overwhelming fear of losing control of oneself. This symptom can be so severe that most who suffer from it feel that they are either dying or losing their mind."

"Which goes back to my comment about the victims killing themselves," interjected Dr. Brown.

Suddenly, the police dispatcher burst through the door without bothering to knock, startling everyone in the conference room. "Sorry to interrupt, but he's on line two!"

"Slow down, Sara! Who's on line two?" said Chief Hart.

"It's him! Your perp!"

"You mean the Omega Killer?" asked Duvall, the words sounding a bit silly coming out of his mouth.

"Yes, sir, and he wants to talk to Officer Barnhill—right now!"

12

Eyebrows shot skyward all over the room. Everyone at the conference table had wanted an inside look into this character, and now they were getting a front-row seat.

"All right, let's get this on speakerphone. I want everyone in here to be silent, except for Officer Barnhill. Not one sound," Duvall instructed. He looked over at Jack, who'd shown no reaction up until now. "You ready for this, Jack?"

"Do I have a choice?"

"It'll be fine. Just keep calm and keep him talking. We need to find out as much as we can about him. What makes him tick. What motivates him. Poise, Jack. That's the name of this game. Okay, here we go. Quiet, everyone." Hardin pointed at Chief Hart, who pressed the button on the intercom and activated it into speaker mode. Wyatt silently jabbed an index finger at Jack, letting him know he was live.

"This is Barnhill."

The garbled voice sounded like some kind of futuristic robot or a bad science fiction movie. "Hello, Jack. Enjoying your homecoming?"

"Yes and no."

"Ah, cryptic, are we? Did you get the poetry I sent you?"

"If you mean the note at my hotel, then yes, I got it."

"So what did you think? How did you like it?"

"Well, I prefer Psalms and Proverbs myself, but then again, they're not so cryptic."

"Touché'. But what's not to understand, Jack? I couldn't have been any more plain."

"The threat against Heather and me—that much I get. It's the rest I'm confused about. What is the red omega supposed to mean? And what does 'face your fears' have to do with *anything*? Is that meant to scare us?"

A scrambled chuckle emanated from the intercom speaker. "Do you *really* think I'm gonna make it that easy for you? Just give you all the answers on a silver platter and then tell the authorities to come and get me? You're smarter than that, Jack."

"Yes, but you wouldn't be playing this game if you didn't want someone else to play along with you. So come on. Let's play."

"That's why I like you, Jack. A logical train of thought. So rare these days. Too many people want to blow things up and ask questions later. It has its merits, but where's the *real* fun in that? Psychological mind games are much more fun. Much more … unpredictable."

"I agree. The real danger is in carrying things too far, past the point of no return. If no one gets why you do what you do, then what's the point of doing it?"

"Are you telling me that my games are an exercise in futility?" asked the voice, a slight annoyance creeping into his tone.

"Is that *your* fear, Mister … by the way, how should I address you?"

"Call me … Omega. The press already does, and I kinda like it. And no, that is *not* my fear! I have no fear of anyone or anything."

"Even if no one decides to play this game with you? That wouldn't concern you at all?"

"No, because these people aren't facing their fears. You'd think they'd have gotten the message, but they haven't. It's like I'm performing a kind of public service, if you will."

"A public service for whom?"

"Why, Jesus, of course, Mr. Biblical Scholar. Doesn't it say in the Good Book that we aren't supposed to be scared of anything? Well, I'm helping Him move things along. Helping people see the light."

"Yes, but—"

"Enough of this talk!" Omega screeched. "I'm not here to argue. I'm here to make you face your fears, Jack."

"I'm not scared of you, Omega."

"I didn't say you were, but I've got a little something that may jar your memory. Maybe your friend Wyatt would enjoy this story too. I know he's right there next to you, along with all the other so-called experts."

Every person in the room exchanged glances with each other, wondering how Omega could have known such a thing. Then again, it was a small town.

Omega cleared his throat and waxed poetic. "The year is 1981. Two of President Reagan's Secret Service agents, Jack Barnhill and Wyatt Hart, drop the ball, neglect their duties, and allow the president of the United States to get shot. Heck, boys, you almost got him killed."

"That's not what happened!" Jack snapped.

"If that's what makes you feel better," said Omega. "If that's what makes it possible for you to sleep at night. Unfortunately, that's not what the report said, did it? If you're not sure, why don't you ask Agent Duvall. It was his twin brother, Hayden, who sold you down the river. Remember?"

"What does that have to do with anything?"

"Blood is thicker than water, Officer Barnhill. You and Wyatt aren't just a *little* concerned about getting railroaded again? If you aren't able to catch me—and you won't—don't you think he'll do the same thing to you two that his brother did in '81?"

The thought planted a seed of doubt in both Jack's and Wyatt's minds, but Jack vehemently denied it. "No, because we're on your trail right now. The point would be moot. He's *not* his brother!"

"Sure does look like him, though. Keep that in the back of your mind. Let the fear sink in a little bit."

"I'm not scared at all."

"Of course you're not, Jack. Maybe you *aren't* as smart as I thought. Remember everything. Forget nothing. Face your fears. See ya!"

"Wait—don't hang up!"

"Gotta go, Jack. Got another lesson in fear to teach. Maybe next time, I'll tell you what the red omega means."

"Wait! Wait! Hello?"

The next sound over the intercom speaker was a dial tone. There was a long moment of silence before someone summoned up the courage to speak.

"We get anything?" Wyatt asked the audio technicians, who had been recording and analyzing the phone conversation from the other side of the conference room wall.

"Voice modification, untraceable phone connection. Basically, we got nothing."

Wyatt dipped his head and then ran a hand across his face in fatigue and frustration. He let out a long audible sigh as Agent Duvall resumed his thoughts.

"I guess we all have a firsthand impression of this guy now. It seems as if everything each one of you folks has said about Omega is true. The question is, what can we do about his arrogance? We *will* take care of this, but only as one. As a team. He is already trying to use our pasts against us, to divide us and to conquer us. He will not! We must not let him. Agreed?" Duvall looked around the room at each person, staring each man directly in the eyes until he nodded in agreement. "Ladies and gentlemen, it's time to 'face our fears.' It's time we became Omega's biggest fear. Let's see if he can practice what he preaches."

$$\Omega$$

The man sat in his SUV, enveloped in the darkness that the heavily tinted windows provided. He'd clicked off his cell phone and tossed it on the passenger seat. He grabbed a set of binoculars and lifted them to his eyes. He'd been watching the couple from the parking lot for nearly thirty minutes. The twentysomethings had been enjoying their day in the park, sprawled out on an old blanket. They'd been sunning themselves, occasionally taking a break to throw around an old Frisbee and imbibe in alcoholic beverages. As the early afternoon marched toward mid-afternoon, the couple's cooler got lighter and lighter as the empty beer bottles started to multiply. The man with the binoculars guessed that they'd had around seven or eight beers each. They'd given up on the Frisbee-tossing and concentrated on each other. The more tipsy they got, the more amorous they became on the blanket.

The man in the SUV was fuming. *The nerve of some people! Behaving in such a manner in a public place. Kids are nearby, for heaven's sake! And on the Lord's day, no less!* He slammed the field glasses down on the seat and then tried to grab them as they bounced onto the floorboard. Cursing as he scooped them up, he knew he'd found his next victim. The level of disrespect for human decency was appalling. He'd check her file one more time to make sure, but he was fairly certain that this was the girl. Omega cranked up the SUV, eager to confirm the woman's medical history and get to work on finding her "cure."

"Enjoy your day, sweetie. Enjoy the wide-open spaces. Sooner or later, you've gotta pay the piper," he mumbled. "Sooner than you think."

13

The six law enforcement officers spent the rest of their day and part of the night engrossed in the details and theories of the previous three murders. They were very slowly but surely making some headway as to what their plan would be. Around eight o'clock, Agent Duvall sent everyone home to get some sleep and refresh their minds. Most were glad to do so, but Chief Hart seemed intent on entrenching himself in his office. Duvall asked Jack to encourage Wyatt to go home, which took some major cajoling. Finally, Wyatt agreed and left the station with Jack around 8:45 p.m. They hopped into Wyatt's pickup and drove through the tiny contingent of persistent reporters still looking for a comment on the cases.

Wyatt flipped open his cell phone and called Annette. "You guys get the guest room set up?" he asked.

"Yes, the CSI team processed the hotel room, so it was in no condition to be stayed in tonight. I'd rather have them stay with us anyway," Annette said with a smile, looking in Heather's direction.

"They probably didn't want to stay there, regardless of the room's condition," Wyatt said. "I wouldn't want them staying there after that last little 'love note.'"

"Heather and I were able to get most of the stuff, and Nick helped us out with the heavier things. They're all moved in, and now we're all one big happy family."

"Well, we're on our way home. We're done for the night. We're waiting on a couple of things from both the GBI and the FBI, but they won't be ready until tomorrow morning."

"There are some leftovers in the fridge, and we popped a bowl of popcorn if you're not very hungry."

"Thanks. We'll find something."

"We'll wait up for you. See you in a few. Love you."

"Love you, too." Wyatt closed his phone and relayed the room-and-board accommodations to Jack.

"Hope we're not imposing on you," said Jack.

"Are you kidding? We *wanted* you and Heather to stay with us, just not under these circumstances," replied Wyatt somewhat incredulously.

"So much for house hunting, though."

"Sorry," shrugged Wyatt.

"It's okay. We know this is where we want to be. I'm glad I'm here, and I hope I'm helping."

"More than you know, brother. More than you know."

"Well, let's remember to keep praying for each other. This won't get any easier as we go, especially without being prayed up."

"You still having your quiet time at night?" asked Wyatt.

"Yep. It's the only time that's good for me. I'm a night owl. I don't function well in the morning, and the times I've tried a morning quiet time, I didn't remember a single verse I read," Jack said almost apologetically.

"I'm just the opposite. I have mine in the morning. I need it to get my day started off right. It gets me in the correct frame of mind to work, so I can give the day to the Lord and let Him work in me."

"The important thing is that we're both getting into the Word and praying. As long as we keep each other accountable, we'll be fine. He will see us though this."

"Amen, Pastor Barnhill! Preach on!" Wyatt laughed.

"I'm only concerned about you, Wyatt. I know you're under a lot of pressure, and I wanna make sure your head's together on this one. Everybody's watching. I want this guy caught almost as much as you do," he said as he patted his friend on the shoulder.

"My one gnawing concern is the other brother."

"Hardin?" asked Jack.

"No, Hayden. I'd like to know how much input he's having with his brother."

"You actually think Hardin would listen to anything Hayden had to say about the cases? It's really none of Hayden's business. He's retired now. Hardin's still in the game."

"I'm talking about us. The Hinckley assassination attempt. We were the fall guys on that one, and it would be just like him to bad-mouth us again. I wonder if he's telling Hardin how we supposedly messed that one up and that he probably shouldn't trust us with this one either," Wyatt replied, pounding the steering wheel for emphasis.

"We didn't drop the ball on that one," Jack insisted

"Yeah, but we got blamed for it, didn't we? He basically ran us out of the Secret Service. Hayden should have told the truth. If he lied then, he'll lie now. He'll say we aren't capable, and Hardin might believe him. Why *wouldn't* he believe his own twin brother?"

"Look, you and I both know that we got jobbed on that one, no pun intended. God knows the truth, and that's all that matters to me. What goes around comes around, so Hayden will have to answer for that one day. Don't sell Hardin short. He has a mind of his own, and he's his own man. Let's give him the benefit of the doubt. I'm not saying we *shouldn't* watch him. I'm not even saying we should totally trust him. Let's cut him a little slack and see if he's got everyone's best interests at heart. If he turns out to be like his brother—"

"Fool me once, shame on you. Fool me twice, shame on me," Wyatt interjected.

"I know, I know. It stretches your limits of trustworthiness when you're not even sure you can trust any of the higher-ups."

"Like the Secret Service ... or the FBI."

"It's not the agencies; it's the individuals. Keep that in mind before you blindly distrust everyone. He's not guilty by association, ya know," Jack told him.

"One more reason for us to pray for each other. I don't like feeling this way. It's not my nature. It's very much out of character for me. I need to know that someone's got my back, and right now the only person I trust with this is you," Wyatt said as he negotiated his truck around a sharp curve.

"What about your guys?" Jack asked. "I understand not trusting Duvall, but you trust your own men, don't you?"

"Yes, but unless they have an alibi, they're suspects too."

"Hmm," said Jack pensively.

"I mean, I trust them. I just can't yet rule them out as suspects. I couldn't tell you where Dr. Brown was on the night of any of these murders. Same with Officer Wayne. I'm pretty sure they didn't do it, but I can't rule them out."

"Plus, they both know me. Whoever's doing this knows who I am, presumably because I used to live here. That doesn't technically rule out Officer Wayne. I knew his father and knew him when he was knee-high to a grasshopper."

Wyatt let out a huge sigh of exasperation as he rounded the corner and drove up Highway 28 toward his home.

"Hey, no frustration now! You're being pulled into his world when you let him get to you like that. He's playing on your nerves … your fears. Do not let him. We'll get him, Wyatt."

They rode on in relative silence except for the hum of the tires on the asphalt. Within a minute or two, they turned off the main highway and onto the gravel drive that led to Chief Hart's home. The headlights bounced over the largely forested area before they beamed onto the modest two-story home up ahead. This house had been the only place Wyatt and Annette had ever lived since they were married. Several repairs and paint jobs, along with a couple of new additions to the home, had kept it from showing its true age. Three outdoor spotlights illuminated the exterior, and a huge motion-activated light clicked on as the vehicle approached the front walkway. Wyatt shoved the gearshift into park and clambered out of the truck. The two men made the short walk up the red brick steps and as if on cue, both heaved a sigh simultaneously. That made them both chuckle.

"It's never easy, is it?" asked Wyatt.

"Well, now where's the fun in that?" Jack responded.

"How do people who don't know the Lord make it?"

"They don't. Sometimes they think they do, but they don't."

"Man, I have the Lord, and it's still hard," Wyatt said as he fumbled with his keys before inserting the correct one into the lock.

Jack nodded, a knowing smile crossing his face. "Yep. I hear ya, brother."

"Welcome to the finish line," Wyatt said as he pushed through the door.

Heather and Annette hopped from their chairs and ushered the men into the kitchen for a quick bite and some small talk before settling in for the night. Jack opted for the ham and Swiss on wheat bread, while Wyatt, still a little upset, munched on a few handfuls of popcorn. The women knew that the men had no desire to talk about the cases, so they entertained them with stories of their move and tales of days gone by. The men smiled and nodded politely as they scarfed down their late supper. Bleary-eyed and exhausted, Jack and Wyatt pushed themselves away from the table and trudged toward their separate rooms, each wife not too far behind them. It had already been a long day, and the days to come promised to be even longer.

14

It was after midnight, and Omega was on the prowl. He'd studied her medical charts. He'd watched her from afar, secretly and stealthily observing every habit and routine. He made sure he knew her schedule, from the number of times she hit the snooze button on her alarm down to the time she turned off the bedroom lamp after falling asleep watching TV. Now it was time for him to make his move. Thursday nights were unofficially the kickoff to the weekend's festivities for the young woman. She frequented one of Valley Springs' two bars, usually with her boyfriend in tow. Her job was like a pressure cooker from morning to night, even though she didn't receive many calls. At least not until recently. She'd only had two calls on this particular day, one a misdial and the other a suspicious person report. It was time to let her hair down. *No more work until Monday,* she thought. *It's party time!*

Omega sat in his SUV a safe distance away from the bar, binoculars in hand. Time was of no consequence to him. He'd sit here and watch her all night if he had to. Cloaked in the darkness of night, his stomach churned in anticipation of his next pupil. His next chance to be the teacher, to help her conquer her fears, wouldn't be very long in coming. In the meantime, his future victim was tucked inside the roadside tavern, indulging herself in way too many beers. The hours had crawled by until her boyfriend and tonight's designated driver decided that she'd had enough for one night.

"C'mon, babe. Let's get out of here. It's almost one in the morning., and I've got to go to work tomorrow."

"Aw, just a couple of more drinks," the young woman slurred. "I'm off 'til Monday. I need to blow off some steam!"

"I know you do, but I've gotta get up early. We can come back tomorrow night."

"No, I wanna stay! You're a party-pooper, you know that?"

"Maybe so, but I've got to earn some money to pay for these drinks. If I don't work, you don't drink."

"Listen here, Mr. Goody Two-Shoes! I earn my own money—"

"Yeah, but you don't pay for the beer. I do. Now, let's go!" He took her by the arm and firmly pulled her to her feet. She barely resisted, stumbling toward the door as her boyfriend paid her tab. The two made their way to her car, the young woman's gait more than unsteady. The boyfriend poured her into the passenger seat and checked his watch—1:07 a.m. *Man, I'm gonna be sleepy in the morning,* he thought. He shoved the keys into the ignition and cranked the engine as the young woman continued to ramble on about having to leave the bar early. He ignored her, his mind choosing to dwell on the fact that he wouldn't be able to sleep late the next morning. In fact, he'd probably be done with lunch before his girlfriend even thought about rolling out of bed. At least he wouldn't have a hangover when he woke up. Sleep deprivation was much less painful. At this point, all he wanted was for her to *not* throw up in the car. Within thirty seconds of driving away, his girlfriend was leaning against the window, sound asleep. He looked over at her and shook his head, oblivious to the fact that he was being followed by a black SUV.

Omega trailed far enough behind the couple so as not to be conspicuous. As the boyfriend maneuvered the car through the streets of Valley Springs and approached his girlfriend's home, she suddenly began to stir from her slumber. Her mouth was pasty and dry, despite her efforts to drink all of the beer in the whole bar. She'd napped with her mouth open, and now her tongue refused to cooperate. Rolling over in the seat, she poked a finger in the air and tried to force out the words.

"Sss … sch … schtop. Wait a minute. Schtop. Stop." The boyfriend glared at her but ignored her protest. She continued. "Stop. Why are you taking me home? I don't wanna go home. I wanna go to your house."

"No, I'm taking you to your house. I've got to wake up early in the morning, and I don't want to disturb your sleep. Plus, if you start getting sick, I don't want you keeping me up. I don't need to hear you upchucking all night."

"I'm not sick! I'm totally fine! I wanna stay with you, baby. I love you. Besides, I'm … I'm schcared," the girl slurred.

"No, you're not scared. You're drunk, and I'm taking you home."

"I *am* scared!" the girl protested. "What about this Omega guy? What if he tries to kill me?" she asked as the crocodile tears started to form.

"He's not gonna get you. I'm not gonna let him. I'll check the house for you, make sure no one's there, and make sure you're all locked in. Heck, I'll even turn down your sheets for you and tuck you in so that you can sleep this one off."

"But … but …" she whimpered in her best drunken sob.

"C'mon, now. Let's go," he said as he pulled the car into her driveway. He jumped out of the driver's seat, circled around to the passenger side, and popped the door handle. He slipped his arm around her waist and escorted her to the front stoop.

She fumbled with her purse in an attempt to dig out her house key and finally produced it after her boyfriend heaved out a huge sigh of frustration. "All right, I've got it! Chill out," she steamed.

He focused on the task at hand, which was to get her in her own bed, make sure she was safe and secure, and get out as quickly as possible. His goal was to be back home and in his own bed by 1:45 a.m. After she'd opened the door, the duo made their way across the living room, down the hall, and into the bedroom. As she flopped down on her bed, the boyfriend removed her shoes and pants and then tucked her underneath the covers.

She was still awake, but just barely. "Make sure I'm locked in, okay?" she mumbled.

"Taking care of it right now."

After he'd secured the house, he crept back into her bedroom to give her a good-night kiss. She was nearly asleep when he gently planted one on her cheek.

She awoke briefly but only to ask a ridiculous question. "Why is this room and my bed spinning?"

The boyfriend laughed as he exited the bedroom and said a quick "I love you" before heading for the front door. He twisted the key in the lock, the last line of defense in the house since she'd not had her alarm properly installed. As he dropped the house key into his pants pocket and spun around, he was met by an axe handle across his forehead. The boyfriend dropped like a bag of rocks and tumbled off the stoop into the flowerbed.

Omega clamped a rag doused in chloroform over the nose of the barely conscious man, further turning out his lights. Hurriedly grabbing the duct tape from his black bag, Omega made quick work of securing the boyfriend. Six revolutions around the ankles, six around the wrists, which had been pulled behind his back, and six around the mouth and eyes, not caring how much hair the boyfriend might lose from his eyebrows and head when he yanked off the tape. *If* he ever yanked off the tape. Right now, the boyfriend was in a bad state of affairs, but he was still alive. Omega flipped him over onto his stomach. He had no intention of killing him—the boyfriend just happened to be in the wrong place at the wrong time. Collateral damage in Omega's greater plan. It could've been worse—at least he wasn't the girl inside.

Omega snatched the spare key she kept hidden underneath the small azalea bush and silently slipped the key into the lock. The door opened, and Omega peered inside. Lights out. No one stirring. Perfect. He stooped down and plucked the blue shoe covers from his bag; then he crept inside. *This one is easy pickings,* he thought as he made his way to the girl's bedroom. The girl put up no resistance to his chloroform rag, as she had already passed out from her over-indulgent night on the town. Omega hoisted her over his shoulder and lugged her back out into the early morning darkness. He slinked his way through an adjacent vacant lot and then across a narrow street and down into a small thicket of pine trees, where he'd left his SUV. Omega went through the same process of duct taping the girl as he had with her boyfriend. Somewhere in the distance, a dog barked as the killer rolled the girl's lifeless body from the tailgate of the SUV into the cargo space. It was showtime. Everything had gone according to plan, except for the boyfriend's unexpected appearance. *Oh well. Next time, I bet he'll duck.*

Omega chuckled at his own twisted attempt at humor. These "truth sessions" always put him in a good mood. *Sooner or later, these people are gonna have to face their fears, and since they won't step up and do it themselves, I'll give them a little "encouragement." They're not gonna find it in any counseling session, any prescription bottle, or at the bottom of a bottle of booze. They've got to find their courage, to step up and face the things that hold them back.*

He smiled at his train of thought as he drove away, with soon-to-be victim number four rolling around in the back of his SUV's cargo hold.

15

Jack and Wyatt were both used to the early morning hours of their jobs but not on this particular morning. Wyatt had tossed and turned all night, sleeping only in fits and starts. Annette was a light sleeper, so Wyatt's insomnia kept her from getting her normal rest as well. Jack and Heather went through a similar scenario in the guest bedroom, but Heather never slept great in a strange bed. Her restlessness contributed to Jack's inability to fall asleep soundly. The four stumbled into the kitchen around 6 a.m., desperately in need of coffee. Annette had already prepared the coffeemaker the night before, so all she had to do was flip on the switch. She shuffled over to the toaster and plopped in four slices of bread. Heather joined in, plucking the jelly and butter from the refrigerator and the honey and peanut butter from the cupboard. Wyatt grabbed the plates, knives, and coffee cups and set them around the table. Meanwhile, Jack checked both men's cell phones for any calls or text messages. Nothing. As he set the phones down on the table, Wyatt's phone began to chirp, startling everyone in the room.

"Hello?" he swiftly answered.

"Good morning, Chief. You boys up and moving?" questioned Agent Duvall.

"Yes, sir. We should be there between 6:30 and 7:00."

"Perfect. We've got a list of people we need to go over, so we'll see you then."

The women allowed the men to pour their coffee and prepare their toast first, so they could leave for the station as soon as possible. The men's hurried pace was in stark contrast to the two women, who could take their time and watch the sunrise wedge its way through the pines. The men gulped down their toast and coffee and then dressed and headed for the door. The darkness was giving way to daylight above the horizon as the two men roared down the road in Wyatt's truck.

"Did you ever think that you'd come home to this?" Wyatt finally asked.

Jack shook his head. "Nope. It never even crossed my mind."

"Breaks my heart. This town may never be the same."

"It's the times we're living in. The big-city stuff eventually trickles down to the small towns too. It's just sad."

When the men reached the police station, the media crews were setting up for their live shots at 7:00, so they hardly noticed when Wyatt's truck pulled through the police barricades and into his designated parking spot. Surprisingly, the men were not ambushed by anyone in the print media as they cruised through the front door.

"Morning, Chief. Morning, Jack," the receptionist said as they breezed through.

"Morning," each replied.

"Agent Duvall's back in the conference room," she announced, motioning behind her.

"Anyone else here yet?" asked Wyatt.

"Not yet. He called everyone on the primary team and told them to be here no later than 7:15."

"Okay. Thanks."

Wyatt and Jack made their way down the hallway, mentally bracing themselves for the information avalanche they assumed was about to move toward them. What they were not prepared for was the sight that awaited them as they opened the conference room door. At the end of the long conference table sat FBI Special Agent Hardin Duvall. Reading his Bible.

Both men stopped short, more than a little shocked and stunned by Duvall's brashness. The surprise must've shown on their faces like spray-painted graffiti, as Agent Duvall let out a short chuckle and motioned for them to come in.

"Good morning, gentlemen. Have a seat." They settled in next to the FBI agent, one on his left and the other on his right. "I brought you guys in a little earlier than the rest. I feel like I owe you an explanation here." Jack and Wyatt exchanged glances as Hardin continued. "Plain and simple, I am *not* my brother. We are identical twins, biologically, but that's where the similarities end. When we were in college, he got his first taste of freedom and ran with it. It was our first real time away from home, away from our parents. I, on the other hand, remained true to my roots, my Christian heritage. A Proverbs 22:6 baby, so to speak."

"Train up a child in the way he should go …" quoted Wyatt.

"Well, I didn't depart from it, praise God," interrupted Hardin, "but I can't say the same for Hayden. College really changed him, changed his heart. He wasn't the same guy I grew up with. The very core of his soul, his being, had mutated. Everything he believed in and stood for was challenged, and he began to doubt himself and his principles. He finally came to the conclusion that just maybe his professors and others with influence over him actually were 'enlightened,' while Mom and Dad knew nothing. He tried to suck me into his little world of deceit and dishonesty, but I didn't bite, praise the Lord."

He paused for a minute to let that sink into their brains at this early hour and then continued. "I said all that to say this: I want to set your minds at ease. You have every right to be apprehensive. I know my brother. I know he set up you guys to take the fall in '81. Please don't let that influence how you feel about me and how you work these cases. I need you two to fully concentrate on everything that's going on, without having to worry about where my loyalties lie. My loyalties are to the FBI in solving these cases, to you guys, and to this." He closed his Bible and held it up for emphasis, shaking it at them as a pastor might when making a very strong point. "Not a lot of people outside of my inner circle at the FBI know of my convictions, but it's not like I'm hiding it either. I'm very open with my faith, but there are people in the bureau who'd love to shut me up."

The three men heard others coming down the hall toward the

conference room. Duvall shoved his Bible into his briefcase and clicked it shut. "Sounds like the rest are here. Anyway, I really wanted to get that off my chest and give you guys some assurances of my loyalty."

The door opened and the rest of the team swept in. Dr. Brown was lugging a stack of files, while Agent Spikes from the GBI and Dr. Sheffield cradled cups of coffee as they quietly chatted. Agent Duvall greeted each of them as they took their places around the conference room table. Wyatt and Jack plopped down, still a little stunned at the proceedings that they'd just experienced.

"All right, everyone's here, so let's begin," Duvall proclaimed. He reached under the table and hauled up a printout about three inches thick. Dropping it on the shiny flat surface, Duvall explained their planned course of action. "We've compiled two lists. The first is of possible victims, based on their medical conditions. Anyone in the Valley Springs area who is being treated for depression, an anxiety disorder, or any type of phobia and is on any type of medication for these disorders is on this list. The second list is of any health care professional who lives or works in Valley Springs. That means doctors, nurses, dentists, pharmacists, or any other specialized field or branch of medicine that falls under the category of health care."

"All those people on that list are from Valley Springs?" asked an amazed Officer Barnhill. "How did you get the authorization on the possible victim's list so easily? Didn't you have to jump through the HIPAA confidentiality hoops to get that info?"

"Ah, the magic of the FBI and a subpoena from a friend of mine, who happens to be one of the most influential judges in the district. There's only one caveat with this list. The subpoena is only for the *rights* to the list. We've got to get the patients to sign a waiver before we're able to talk to them."

"So how do we split this up?" asked Chief Hart.

"I want to send the medical people, meaning Dr. Brown and Dr. Sheffield, to talk to the anxiety patients and collect their waivers. I'll speak as to how we want to do that in just a minute. Special Agent Spikes and

Chief Hart will tackle the medical professions list. You guys have eight doctors' offices and one hospital by my count; isn't that right, Chief?"

"Yes, that's correct."

"Okay. Officer Barnhill and I will stay here and check off the names as you guys call them in, work any new leads we may get, and do all the administrative stuff."

"How many names are we talking about?" asked Agent Spikes.

"Four hundred and eight, total, and that includes active, inactive, and retired personnel. Dr. Brown and Dr. Sheffield have 258 patients to track down, and you have the balance of that number, Martin."

Agent Duvall broke down exactly how he wanted each person questioned and what to look for in his or her response. Each one with a corroborated alibi would get marked off the list, and each patient who seemed particularly vulnerable would be watched more carefully by the police cruisers on neighborhood patrol. It would be a long and arduous task, but to Jack, Wyatt, and all the other residents of Valley Springs, the tedium of the job was worth the assurance that Omega would soon be behind bars.

Ω 16

It was your everyday, run-of-the-mill chest freezer. A little over three feet tall. Small but with plenty of room for storing extra deer meat or bags of ice. Today, it held a different treasure. The woman began to stir after her combination bender/chloroform rag to the face. Her eyes were trying to adjust to the darkness when she sensed a sliver of light from outside her vault shining through a tiny crack in its lid, directly into her pupils. She jerked her head, heavy with a hangover, away from the brightness but it illuminated a far larger problem. Just in front of her, maybe a foot from her face at the most, was a wall. It was awfully close. Uncomfortably close. She tried to push herself away from the wall with her feet, but her ankles had been taped together. The girl tried to free her legs, but all she could feel was the stickiness of the duct tape threatening to take off her top layer of skin. She wiggled her wrists slightly. They were duct taped too. *Where am I?* she thought. She felt horrible from the late night of drinking, but this was a different type of feeling. She was … cramped. The girl tried to adjust her position by attempting to roll over onto her left hip. A loud clattering sounded behind her. *What was that?* Now she was stuck on her left hip, unable to move. Her eyes darted about, and her breathing became more shallow and labored. *Oh, no! Don't panic! Don't panic! Don't panic!* she kept repeating in her mind. It was too late. Her body was already in knots. Her stomach was churning, partially from the anxiety, partially from the drinking binge. Her head had begun to throb, and her body ached. *Who did this? Where am I? I need my Xanax! I'm freaking out here!* The young woman's mind was in overdrive as she tried to cope with her situation and figure out where she was. She couldn't see anything, but it seemed to her that the walls around her were closing in quickly. The back of her head, her feet, and her left shoulder were jammed against some kind of cold, hard barrier. *Whatever I'm in, it's not much bigger than me. I've gotta get out of here!* The blackness that surrounded her now had enveloped her mind. She desperately tried to piece it all together. The best she could figure, she was trapped in a cramped box, unable to move, and with no way out. Even worse, she could tell she was starting to have a severe panic attack. Between her attempts at exhaling slowly, she cried out at the top of her lungs. *Now I really can't breathe! Help me! Oh, God! Help me!* After what seemed like an eternity for her (but was actually less than five minutes), she stopped screaming and tried to take another breath when she heard a ringing sound. *What was that?* It continued to ring. *Is that … a cell phone?*

She wasn't far off the mark. It wasn't *a* cell phone; it was hundreds of cell phones, all ringing at the same time. All around her, the beeping and chirping bounced loudly off her eardrums. The light of the phone keypads illuminated her surroundings—and she finally realized she was being held captive in an old chest freezer. That made her claustrophobic enough. Then she made the strange discovery that she was buried up to her neck in ringing cell phones and her wrists and ankles were duct-taped together. The combination of these two predicaments set her brain buzzing and her nerves even more on edge. Her head throbbed with the pain of a hangover, made even worse by the chirping of hundreds of phones. No matter how hard she tried, no matter the direction she thrashed her body, the woman could not hit the *talk* button to stop even one of the phones from ringing. But how could all the phones be ringing? Were they all programmed with the same phone number? Who could have done this? Immediately, she felt the air being sucked from her lungs. The panic attack had set in! The cold hard truth of her predicament descended on her like a hawk on a field mouse. No inhalers. No antidepressants. No anti-anxiety medications. Her mind dwelled on that fact for a few seconds, sending her mentally spiraling into despair and hopelessness. As she thrashed around inside the freezer and attempted to scream once again, her eyes were drawn to one particular cell phone. The cell phone had been purposely taped to the inside of the freezer door. The caller ID kept flashing one word: OMEGA. The phone was low enough for the girl to activate it by hitting it with her head. In her terror, she lurched toward the freezer's lid. Luckily, her right shoulder struck the *talk* button on the keypad, setting the phone into answer mode. Omega could hear the clattering of cell phones, the thumping of body parts against the freezer, and the gasping and wheezing of his latest victim. The speaker phone was on and functioning. Omega let out a soft chuckle as he listened to his victim struggle—right beneath him. The young woman heard his laugh and suddenly, all the phones stopped ringing … and she realized that someone was out there, listening to her. Laughing at her.

"Help! Help me! Please! Help me! Help!"

"I've thought it through … and I'm afraid the answer is no," declared Omega.

"Please, help me! I'm trapped inside this freezer! You've gotta help me! Please! I … I can't breathe!"

Omega calmly sat on top of the freezer's lid, cross-legged, like an Indian in front of his tepee. "Stop making all that noise down there. You're making it impossible for me to think. I'm trying to figure out what to do with you. Besides, you're running out of air in there. Don't you feel the walls closing in on you?"

The girl's wheezing began to deepen and grow louder with each attempt to inhale. She banged her head against the lid in frustration and desperation. Omega raised his voice and said, "God didn't give you a spirit of fear, my dear. But then again, what do you know about God? You certainly won't find Him carousing in a bar. So what is it that makes you drink so much? Do you have something to hide? What are you scared of? It's time to face your fears, and since you won't do it on your own, I'm afraid I'm going to have to help you." Omega snickered at his choice of words.

Her heart felt as if it would pound out of her chest, and she was dangerously close to hyperventilating. Her lungs were pumping furiously, trying to pull in a volume of air. She was teetering on the edge of blacking out when she heard Omega hang up the phone, only to punch in more numbers and make another call. He placed the party on speaker phone, then turned up the volume on the keypad loud enough for his victim to hear. The voice on the other end of the line was a familiar one—a coworker of hers.

"9-1-1. What is the nature of your emergency?"

"Um, yes. I'd like to report a 9-1-1 operator, please."

"I'm sorry, sir. Can you repeat that?"

"One of your coworkers is really attached to her job, so much so that she's literally surrounded herself with phones. She's buried herself in her work, in a sense. She just can't seem to break away."

The girl's thrashing and heavy breathing could be heard through Omega's phone and alarmed the operator, who motioned for her supervisor to trace the call. "I think I hear her, sir," she said.

"Yes, you do," Omega shot back. "She's quite distracting when she's hyperventilating."

"She's hyperventilating?"

"Yes, and it's quite frustrating. I'm trying to conduct a telephone conversation with you, and she just won't shut up. She's not very cooperative that way. Anyway, as I was saying, she's a fellow 9-1-1 operator, and I'm hoping for her imminent success in overcoming these personal demons of hers. Her fears. I'm sad to report that it doesn't appear to be working out, so I'm gonna make her conquer them."

"Can you tell me where she is?"

"Yeah, she's sitting in a freezer directly underneath me. And she's hyperventilating, by the way."

"No, I mean can you give me your exact address?"

"I could, but where's the fun in that?"

"Sir, are you able to render aid to her?"

"Well, no. I can't render aid. Kinda defeats my purpose here. However, this young woman can help me and help herself by doing just one thing. Face … her … fears."

There was a short moment of silence while the operator checked with her supervisor. The phone trace still hadn't been picked up. She would have to keep him talking. Omega interrupted the brief silence.

"I can see that you're gonna be no help at all. I've got two 9-1-1 operators and both of them are useless. I'll call someone who I know will help me."

"Sir, let me—"

"Stop calling me 'sir'! I haven't been knighted lately! Now, can you connect me to Officer Jack Barnhill at the Valley Springs Police Department, or do I have to hang up on you and do it myself?"

17

The list was overwhelming, even for such a small town. Doctors Brown and Sheffield had the toughest part. Much of the work they had to do would require them to go door-to-door, seeking permission to discuss that individual person's medical condition. Not an easy sell by any means. Because Dr. Brown doubled as a family practice physician in Valley Springs, he was more likely to receive cooperation from the townspeople, especially from those who were already his patients. The two doctors had talked about possibly splitting the list of 258, but most people would probably not be as willing and open to chat about their health care with a total stranger like Dr. Sheffield. They decided that tandem questioning would be the best option. One doctor would discuss the medical history, while the other would collect the signed waivers and consent forms. To break the monotony, Dr. Brown would interview the patients from his own practice, and Dr. Sheffield would speak to those who saw other doctors. They estimated the time it would take to see everyone on their list to be anywhere from ten days to two weeks, if all went according to plan. Some of the more familiar and somewhat surprising names on the list included the mayor of Valley Springs, who was being treated for agoraphobia, the fear of being in a crowded place.

As for the health care professionals, Special Agent Martin Spikes of the Georgia Bureau of Investigation and Chief Hart deduced that the best time to catch a large number of doctors or nurses was during the lunch hour between noon and 1 p.m. They would try to tackle a couple of the doctors' offices around that time and save the early mornings and late afternoons for the dentists, pharmacists, and retired professionals. Their primary objective was to find anyone who had access to midazolam. Logically, they could eliminate the doctors who didn't perform any kind of surgical procedures, thus having no need for the drug. However, they could leave no stone unturned and had to ask even the most obvious questions. That would include the questioning of one of their own, Dr. London Brown, and his assistants, many of whom were helping them with these particular cases. They would also have to interrogate Officer Nick Wayne, who had some EMT training in his background. The one name on the list that shocked both Sparks and Hart was Pastor Noel Marshall, who'd been an assistant to the medic as well as a chaplain in the army, decades ago. In all the time he'd known Pastor Marshall, Wyatt never knew that he'd been a medical assistant in the army. He'd known of his army commitment but figured Marshall had been a chaplain only.

Agent Duvall and Detective Barnhill were at the station house, cross-referencing both lists. Since they knew that Omega was preying on the phobias of the townspeople, the men looked at other diagnoses, specifically those that Omega had not yet brought to light. He'd already exposed those who were being treated for acrophobia, arachnophobia, and ophidiophobia. He'd shown that his victims were vulnerable, that they couldn't face their fears. Worse yet, he'd shown no signs of stopping his game of terror, but Hardin and Jack weren't about to let him run rampant through Valley Springs. As the two scanned the roster of names, they detected several people who had a duplicate phobia with someone who'd already been murdered. Those people were marked off the master list. According to Agent Duvall's FBI profiling expertise, there was no reason to think the killer might command a repeat performance with the same phobia. He was more into teaching one particular person a lesson and then letting the others with that same phobia snap into line. Jack and Hardin continued to pare down the list until they'd reached four new phobias that Omega had not yet shined his twisted light of truth upon. A total of eleven patients in all. Now the hard part would be to get a waiver from those eleven, even though it was for their own good, for their own safety. More than likely, these were Omega's next targets—and they needed to be protected.

$$\Omega$$

Ten hours of digging later, as the day was speeding toward dusk, Agent Duvall called everyone back to the station for the night. Doctors Brown and Sheffield had eliminated quite a few suspects and had picked up the list of eleven from Hardin and Jack. Chief Hart and Agent Spikes also had trimmed away nearly half of their list. They had yet to speak to Dr. Brown or his staff but hoped they would soon be eliminated as suspects. As they were finishing their list comparisons and gathering up their belongings, the night receptionist buzzed over the intercom, startling everyone in the conference room with the urgency of her tone. "Sir, it's him! It's Omega, and he wants to speak to Detective Barnhill."

The room snapped to attention as Duvall gave the okay to push the call through.

"Why is he asking for me now?" huffed Jack. "I've been here all day."

"Just talk to him. Get *something* out of him," said Duvall.

"I'll do what I can," Jack replied and pointed to the phone. Hardin released the hold button and silently backed away. "Detective Barnhill speaking."

"Jack, my old friend. I knew you'd be there. Working on any new leads? You guys getting closer to tracking me down?"

Jack met his taunts with a stony silence, refusing to acknowledge Omega.

"You're no fun, Jack! You don't get my jokes! No matter. I've got a few things to say, and you're just the person I wanted to talk to," spat Omega.

"Go ahead. I'm listening."

"Well, I'm glad *someone's* listening. It surely wasn't the 9-1-1 operator that I tried speaking with a few minutes ago."

"Why did you call the operator, Omega?" Jack asked warily.

"I think you know why, Jack."

"Why don't you enlighten me. Here's your chance to humor me a little. It's been a very long day."

"Ah, Jack," Omega chuckled, sounding even stranger with the voice modifier attached to the phone, "don't you remember my mantra? Now gather everyone around you in the room, and let's all say it together. Ready? One … two … three. Face your fears. Once again, Jack, there are people out here who don't believe lard is greasy, if you know what I'm saying."

"People aren't taking your warnings seriously. Is that what you're trying to say?"

"You see, Detective, if everyone was as intelligent as you, we wouldn't be having this problem."

Jack pressed his ear closer to the phone. He could hear a thumping in the background. "I guess I'm not that smart. What is that noise I'm hearing? I can't figure it out."

"Oh, that's my friend here. She's just chilling, as the kids say. She's just … kicking it."

"When you say 'kicking it'—"

"Not the bucket, Jack. At least not yet. That totally depends on her—and you guys. She's in good company, though. She's got the same problem that plagued Houdini, Hitler, and your old pal Ronald Reagan. Basically, I've got a young lush here, and the poor wench has claustrophobia. That's why I've got her stuffed in this freezer until she … well, you know. I don't feel like repeating myself anymore."

"Talk to me, Omega. How do we keep her alive?"

"Very noble, Jack, but she's got to do this on her own since her own belief in God is, shall we say, waning."

"You're right, Omega. We can't depend on others for our own redemption. That's between us and God. But it doesn't sound like you're giving her too much of a chance to redeem herself. Are you in this for the thrill of the kill? Is it just one big game to you, or do you really think you're 'helping God along,' as you said? Because the God I believe in offers redemption. You don't. So how can you be doing His work?" A long silence ensued. Jack spoke up again to make sure the phone line hadn't gone dead. "Hello? Are you still there?"

"I'm here! Where else would I go, you twit!" Omega roared.

Jack knew he had touched a nerve. He'd ruffled the feathers of Omega's normally calm and calculated dialogue. Hardin quickly scribbled out a note urging Jack to apologize. "I'm sorry, Omega. I think I might have carried things a little too far."

"Me, too. I think I gave this girl too much epinephrine. She won't shut up!"

"Let's concentrate on her for a second. Tell us where she is. She needs help, and since I'm a believer, let me personally help her."

"You know, Jack, I might just let you do that. I know you and Chief Hart are legit. You talk the talk and walk the walk, so I just might give you a small hint. One problem, though. You'd better hurry. She's getting awfully quiet in there."

Everyone in the conference room had noticed that there wasn't as much background noise bleeding through the speaker phone. Hardin made a circular motion with his right hand, signaling Jack to keep Omega talking.

"Okay. That's good. Thank you."

Omega huffed out one long sigh and then delivered his response. "There are four places in this town, other than your station house or any place that deals with retail frozen food, like a grocery store or convenience store, where you can find a chest freezer. When you name one of the four, I'll let you know. When you get to the fourth, I'll hang up. You'll have it figured out by then. Just to make it interesting, and since I know this is a party line, I'll call on each of you. Kinda like *Family Feud*. Let's start with you, Jack. Name one place where you'll find a chest freezer."

"A restaurant, like Mama K's," said Jack.

"Ding! That's one. Chief Hart, I know you're out there. What's your answer?"

"Uh, how about in people's homes? Lots of people around here have an extra ice chest," Wyatt replied, sounding very unsure of himself.

"Ding! Very nice, Chief. Two down, two to go. What say you there, Agent Duvall? Got any guesses?"

"The appliance store downtown on Main Street."

"Ding! That makes three. Any of you other three care to take a stab at the fourth answer?"

Agent Spikes, Dr. Sheffield, and Dr. Brown looked around at each other, trying to decide who would offer up an answer to Omega. Suddenly, Dr. Brown's eyes lit up as the answer streaked across his brain like a lightning bolt. As soon as it appeared in his mind, it burst from his lips. "The taxidermist out on Bayline Highway!"

Click.

Agent Duvall leapt from his chair, knocking it over in the process. He barked out orders over his walkie-talkie. "I need two squad cars to Lynn's Taxidermy on Bayline! Suspect is on the move, but victim may still be there. Hurry, boys! We're on our way, too. Be careful going in there."

Before Duvall could hear the affirmative response, the six had piled into the FBI-issued SUV and were roaring toward the outskirts of Valley Springs. They would have to hurry to make it in time to save the girl—or to catch Omega.

18

The look on their faces said it all. The group of six sprang from the vehicle, almost before it had come to a complete stop. However, they pulled up short in the dizzying red and blue strobe lights as the officers who arrived first on the scene emerged from the building, shaking their heads. Another victim. Duvall slammed his hand in frustration on the hood of the SUV. They hadn't made it in time, not that Omega had given them much of a chance anyway. The girl was dead, and Omega was gone. Agent Duvall and Chief Hart pushed their way through the door and then made a hard left toward the processing area. The others trailed behind them, carefully looking for anything that might help with the case. Chief Hart was met by Officer Nick Wayne, who had been on duty and was one of the first officers there.

"She's in that cooler," Officer Wayne pointed to the box in the corner, "but it's been unplugged for a while, so it's not even cold. We know her, Chief. It's Tracy from Emergency Services. She's a 9-1-1 dispatcher. She's been dead a little less than an hour."

Duvall and Hart peered into the cooler at the lifeless body as Jack stepped up beside them. The girl was rolled into the fetal position, legs tucked tightly underneath her. Her pale complexion was spattered with small dots of what appeared to be blood. Whether it was from the cooler, the girl, or Omega himself was what the forensics team was now trying to determine. There were several small cuts and bruises covering her body, presumably from her attempts to free herself. She'd left several dents on the inside cover of the freezer as she'd tried to kick her way out, to no avail. Other than that, the men could see no other signs of physical trauma. It appeared to be another death caused by a claustrophobia-induced panic attack. It definitely looked like the work of Omega. The index card on the top of the lid confirmed it.

NOT EVEN 9-1-1 CAN SAVE YOU.
FACE YOUR FEARS.

The red symbol was right in the center of the card, exactly where it always was. What was this fascination with the Greek letter omega? Why was it red? Why did every index card message end with the words 'Face Your Fears'? Omega was taunting them now. He'd escalated the killings, going from the general public to law-enforcement officials. He'd already made a veiled threat against Jack and Heather. The difference was that the 9-1-1 operator had been clinically diagnosed with claustrophobia-induced panic disorder and was being treated with medication when she wasn't on duty. Jack had no such problem. He'd always had nerves of steel. He'd never feared anything in his adult life, and the killer had to know that. This one thought ran through Jack's mind and only confirmed his suspicion that he and Omega were linked somewhere in their past. The only way the killer could get to him was if he somehow knew Jack's latent fear. Agent Duvall's voice snapped him away from his thoughts.

"All right, we're gonna put out a call to stop and check every vehicle from now until 7:00 a.m. Anyone traveling within the county line is automatically pulled over. No exceptions. If Omega hasn't made it home or left the county by now, we'll get him. He should still have the tools of his 'trade' in the car with him. Call in everyone from local enforcement. Agent Spikes, can we get more state patrolmen down here ASAP?"

"Consider it done," Spikes replied.

"Dr. Brown, Dr. Sheffield, I want you to do a quick rundown on the crime scene and then get yourselves home and get some sleep. You're no good to me if you're not rested. You've gotta be fresh to be able to think the way I need you to think. Leave your notes with Agent Spikes before you go home. Call me if you get anything big. We'll crank it up at the same time tomorrow morning. The rest of you, come with me." Hardin made a beeline for the SUV with Jack, Wyatt, and Agent Spikes in tow, looking like a mother duck leading her ducklings. He slammed the gas pedal to the floor, shooting gravel from under the car's tires.

He addressed his troops as he careened toward the police station. "This conversation stays in this car. If it gets out, it'll be bad PR for us. Plus, I'll know where the leak originated. I'm thinking we need to concentrate more on the possible suspects and less on who the next victim might be. I know that sounds cold, but it's the fastest and best way we can get this creep off the streets, in my opinion. We can't worry about the potential victims. They can stay in and lock their doors, listen to the news, whatever they have to do to cope. Bottom line: tracking Omega down is job number one. We've gotta get into his head somehow, make him slip up and make a mistake. He seems to relate better to Jack and Wyatt, so you two will run point on any conversations with Omega. We need to find out how to contact him, rather than waiting on him to get in touch with us. The main thing we need to try to figure out is what motivates him. Is it a hatred for people in general? Is it revenge for some slight committed in the past? Does he not like Christians or non-Christians?"

"He seems to quote a lot of Scripture, but his actions aren't matching his words," said Chief Hart. "He's all about making people face their fears, because it doesn't fit in with what God says about fear. The thing is, his heart has it all wrong. He may want to see people be more like God, but he's got a warped way of making them conform. He's forcing them, not letting them make the choice themselves. He's taking free will completely out of the picture."

"Exactly," chimed in Jack. "You saw what happened when I pushed him about doing God's work? He snapped! He's not interested in redemption at all. He's lying to himself and to us. He's more interested in revenge."

"Well, he got it a few minutes ago with Tracy, didn't he?" Hardin observed. That brought the conversation in the car to a sobering halt. All the theories and philosophies stopped whenever a dead body was involved, especially a law enforcement officer's dead body. The truth of a dead body trumped any kind of idealistic mind game that one chose to believe in.

"Sorry about the candid analysis, but we're all feeling the pressure a little bit," Hardin resumed. "Focusing on Omega is the key to this. We're in a fishbowl. The public is watching us, the media is watching us, and the townspeople are watching us. That's just the facts, guys. We can't let this get our minds in a vise grip. We focus, and we deal with it. Focus on Omega and nothing else."

Ω

The pine trees that bordered both sides of the drive stood like sentinels, the tips of their branches pointing skyward like muskets. They stood watch over the small two-bedroom brick home, spreading out and surrounding it on all sides like a mini-fortress. The only things that intruded on this little slice of wilderness heaven were the occasional herd of deer or a random bobcat. The crickets chirped their peaceful songs, oblivious to the activity nearby. It was a scene of peace and quiet. Too bad the serenity didn't spill over into the heart of the man who lived here. Omega slid the vehicle to a stop thirty feet from his house. His driveway was an old country-style red clay track. The winding dirt path had been worn by years of car tires rolling over its surface. A strip of grass about a foot wide ran right down the middle of the pathway. There were numerous small potholes that dotted its entire quarter-mile length. Some days it made for a fun ride home, kind of like a roller coaster, especially if he drove a little too fast. Today was not one of those days. Omega grabbed the black bag containing the used syringes, the chloroform rags, and the duct tape, and sprinted toward the darkness of his backyard. Rounding the corner of the carport, he reached up with his left hand and flipped on the floodlight. The sudden illumination sent a small creature, either a raccoon or an opossum, scurrying into the woods. He dropped the bag onto the ground and unzipped it. In the right corner of his backyard stood a fire pit shaped like a small chimney. He gathered the syringes, the rag, and the shoe covers he was still wearing and tossed them onto a pile of slightly charred logs. He kept a small bottle of lighter fluid and a disposable lighter under a nearby shrub.

Quickly checking his surroundings, he used the lighter fluid to heavily douse the items and the logs. Two flicks of the flint wheel and the fire pit was awash in a bright orange flame. The fire shot up through the timber and licked at the articles resting on top. Smoke billowed out of the top of the pit, giving the surrounding area an eerie grayish haze. Once he was satisfied that the evidence was sufficiently consumed, Omega turned toward the house and left the fire to burn out on its own. He reached under a small window ledge and produced the key to the side door. After unlocking the door, he pushed his way in, flipped on the light, and tossed the key onto a nearby table. The place was spotless. Freshly scrubbed floors left a slightly flowery scent in the air. Nothing seemed amiss or out of place. Not bad for a man who lived alone. A certified bachelor who had never married and didn't like pets, Omega had become quite comfortable with his lifestyle. He reached into the refrigerator and plucked out a container of strawberry yogurt and a carton of orange juice. After pouring himself a large glass of juice, he grabbed a spoon. A bunch of bananas on the kitchen table caught his eye, so he picked one from the bunch and took it with him to the den. He plopped into an oversized recliner and pulled up the footrest. The remote control sat on a nearby end table, and Omega pressed the power button as he settled into his chair. He tore the lid from the yogurt container, peeled the banana, and dug in. It was time for his favorite news show. At this point, all of the newscasts were his favorite. He was the star of the show, the featured attraction. His handiwork was on display for the whole world to see. And that was just the way he liked it.

19

They were holed up in the conference room, bleary-eyed and exhausted. It had been nearly twenty-four hours since any of them had slept. Fresh pots of coffee were percolating, giving the entire police complex a wonderful aroma. Agent Duvall could tell that his troops were starting to sag, even with the adrenaline rush of the last murder scene. No amount of black coffee would keep them awake until morning broke.

"Guys, I know this thing is fresh, but we've gotta send some of you home. We need well-rested brains on this case at all times. Brown and Sheffield are already home, but one or two of you need to go get some sleep as well. I'll ask for volunteers and if I don't have any, I'll make an executive decision."

A typical lawman response occurred. Not a soul was willing to give up or give in, no matter how tired they were. No one was going to step up and volunteer.

"Okay. This doesn't reflect on anyone here, so don't take it personally. Agent Spikes, I'm picking you to be first. We need an authority figure here when and if something breaks, and I happen to be asleep. I can make it until noon at least, so why don't you get out of here and relieve me around twelve or so?"

"Sounds good," replied Spikes, somewhat reluctantly.

"Chief Hart, Detective Barnhill. You got it in you to hang with me until noon?"

"As long as the coffee's here, I'm here," mumbled Jack.

"Noon? Is that all you've got left in you?" Wyatt said with a smirk.

"All right, for the next twenty-four hours we work in shifts of three,"

Duvall announced. "Spikes, Brown, and Sheffield will cover us until 6:00 or so tonight; then we'll work until we catch Omega or until our eyelids won't stay open. The next day, we'll all get back together as one group. Okay, that's it."

Agent Spikes dragged himself away from the table and wearily made his way toward his cruiser. Chief Hart retrieved a coffeepot and some day-old pastries that had been left in the reception area.

Hardin and Jack sat at the table, shuffling papers about, sifting through the notes, looking for any piece of evidence they might have missed before. The more they stared at them, the more the pages seemed to blur together. It became a huge source of frustration, especially since they were so fatigued.

Jack pushed away from the table and looked skyward, his bloodshot eyes staring directly into the fluorescent lights. He muttered a quick prayer barely loud enough for anyone to hear. "Lord, help us. We can't do this without You. Show us the way."

"Can I get a witness?" Agent Duvall replied.

"Sorry. Just getting a little frustrated, that's all. Seems like we put out a fire in one spot and another fire pops up in a different spot."

"We call it 'running in place' at the Bureau."

"You get to a point where you see the same things over and over, and there's no new angle, no fresh set of eyes to sift through the evidence and see it in a whole new light," Jack said wearily.

"That's where patience comes in. That's the hardest part for me personally, to be still and listen," said Duvall as Chief Hart re-entered the room, coffeepot in one hand and danish in the other.

"I need my patience in a hurry!" Wyatt interjected with a weak smile.

"I'm the same way, but God is teaching me to listen," Duvall said. He says in Psalms 46 to be still and know that He is God. I've gotta do my part and listen. I can't try to do things all on my own, even though my human side seems to think that I can. Isaiah once said that they who wait upon the Lord shall renew their strength. Right now, we all need His strength."

"Not only are you an FBI agent, but you're a regular Old Testament prophet too," joked Jack as he reached for the danish tray.

The three men sat at the table and talked about their relationship with Jesus, trying their best to let their brains unwind a little bit. They all knew that if they didn't lean totally on Him, the stress of these cases would eat them alive. As they continued to fellowship, they could hear the television trucks rumbling in to set up for the morning's live remotes. With the noise of the trucks as a backdrop, the men gradually turned their conversations toward Omega. How was it that this one sick, sadistic monster had turned the town totally upside down in the space of just a few short weeks? That was the overriding question that they were left to answer. Everyone was depending on them. They had to come through, and they would but only with the Lord's help.

$$\Omega$$

News traveled fast, especially in a small town. The 9-1-1 operator's death put an exclamation point on the shock wave that had been reverberating around Valley Springs for over two weeks. If the killer was brash enough to go after law enforcement officers, then who would be able to stop him from coming after them? The thought had most people locking their doors and drawing the shades. They had become prisoners in their own town. Fear had gripped their hearts and minds, and that was exactly what Omega *didn't* want. This only angered him more, that these "God-fearing" people were not putting their trust in Jesus. Instead of facing their fears, they were playing duck-and-cover. Their mouths said one thing, but their actions said something totally different. *Hypocrites!* he thought. Religious scholars liked to throw this particular word around with abandon, but in this case, it really rang true. It was always easy to trust Him in the good times when things were okay, but what did most people do when things were not so good? Where did their faith go? Did they blame God? Most of them took a defeatist attitude and wallowed in the mire of self-pity. Omega was determined to change this mind-set, even if he had to kill the whole town of Valley Springs to do it.

$$\Omega$$

"This is Amanda Sutter, reporting live from Valley Springs, Georgia, where a fourth victim of the Omega Killer has been discovered. The body was found late last night after an anonymous phone tip led law enforcement officials to a local business, where they found the body of the young woman. She was pronounced dead on the scene. An autopsy is scheduled for later this morning. The victim was a member of the Valley Springs emergency services department, where she served as a 9-1-1 operator. Her name is being withheld until next of kin are notified. There have been unofficial reports that her boyfriend may have also been a target of the killer but somehow managed to escape harm. We'll update you as soon as we know more information. Reporting live from Valley Springs police headquarters, this is Amanda Sutter. Back to you guys in the studio."

$$\Omega$$

"We need to have the press conference as soon as possible, or it's only going to get worse. We'll throw the media a small bone, give them a little something to chew on for a while. Chief, you and I will handle that one. We'll schedule it for 6:00 p.m., but we'll take our time and get out there closer to 6:30. We won't give up very much. Basically, our story will be that we're working on leads, with several suspects in mind that we will be bringing in for questioning. Obviously, we won't give names, but we're going to continue to work our lists when we can. Eventually, we *will* take our suspects from there, but the media doesn't need to know that right now. Give them just enough to run with, and that'll keep them busy until we get something a little more concrete."

Agent Duvall continued to plot out the administrative points in dealing with both the print and television media. It was a necessary evil, and it bridged the gap between their conversation about Jesus and their impending decision as to who would be the next name pared from their master list. As he slogged through the painstaking details, his cell phone began to vibrate in his pocket. A voice he hadn't heard in quite a while was on the other end—his brother. He excused himself from the room to take the call. "Hello, Hayden."

"Hardin, I know you're extremely busy. I just wanted to let you know I'm here in town, working as an expert analyst on TVBN. Anything I can do for you—"

"Then you know that I can't say anything to you about the cases, so don't even ask," Hardin fired back, angered that his own twin brother could possibly be hurting his cases by playing devil's advocate with the media. Conflict of interest apparently had never entered his brother's mind.

"Whoa, brother! I was just calling to give you a heads-up, that's all. I figured it was the fair thing to do. Don't bite my head off about it!"

"Why would you do any kind of consultant work on any case, *especially* this case? You should be somewhere warm, catching fish, at this point in your life. Aren't you supposed to be retired? Do you need the money that bad?"

"No, I don't need the money. However, TVBN is paying me quite well, so don't knock it until you've tried it. Besides, I need to be in the game somehow. Retirement is boring me to tears."

"But why *this* case, Hayden? You know there's a lot of history here, especially with—"

"Let me stop you right there, Hardin. TVBN approached *me*. I didn't approach them. They knew I had a history with Chief Hart and Detective Barnhill that went all the way back to the Reagan days."

"Then you should have had the good sense to turn down their offer. It makes you look like you still have it in for them. And maybe for me."

"Now you're just being paranoid!"

"Am I? Put yourself in my shoes! Now, how would you feel?"

"Listen, I know that Wyatt and Jack have made their fair share of mistakes, but I'm not going to hold their pasts against them!"

"*If* they made a mistake during the Reagan thing, it was only because they had poor leadership!"

"Okay, that was uncalled for! Consider this your warning. I'm gonna tell the truth. I'm gonna call a spade a spade. You won't be getting any special treatment because you happen to be my brother. If you mess up—"

"I'm sure you'll be all too glad to be there to inform the nation," Hardin interrupted. "How noble of you!"

"If I were one of your 'religious' friends, I'd pray for you. How you're going to clear these cases with those two screw-ups backing you up is beyond me."

"Well, that's your problem right there. You don't have faith in anybody or anything, except yourself."

"We'll see about that. Keep telling yourself that God's going to bail you out, and you'll end up like them," Hayden sniped.

"You mean happy and content with my life? Living for Jesus? Or living like you?"

Hardin knew he'd touched a nerve when he heard the line go dead. *So be it*, he thought. *I have cases to solve.* And now he was more motivated and determined than ever to do so. He slipped back into the conference room, adrenaline pumping. "All right, fellas. Let's get to it."

Deep down inside, Hardin Duvall's heart was breaking.

Ω20

The rest of the morning was a blur, with the three men planning the press conference while simultaneously fighting off exhaustion and watching the clock. Shortly before noon, a bleary-eyed Agent Spikes came in to relieve the others. Dr. Sheffield was next to arrive, minutes before Dr. Brown. Before the three men left, they updated the others who had just come in on their progress and the press conference scheduled for later that day. Dr. Brown gave them a quick rundown on the toxicology: the same combination Omega had used in each case. No new surprises. No new ground broken.

The men slipped out a rear exit in order to avoid unnecessary media attention. Wyatt and Jack made their way back to the Harts' home, each one quickly carrying on a short conversation with his wife before heading straight to bed. Neither one of them stirred from their slumber until the alarm went off around 5:15 p.m. Jack made a dash for the shower, while Wyatt fixed himself a quick bite to eat. They reversed places fifteen minutes later and then hopped into Wyatt's truck around 5:50. On the drive in, Wyatt's cell phone began to buzz. Agent Duvall's name lit up the caller ID. "Hello?"

"Pulling into the police station now. You boys on the way?" Duvall asked.

"Yes, sir. We're about five minutes away. How's the media crush looking?"

"Oh, just being typical press. They're swarming around everywhere like ants to a doughnut."

"Everything ready?"

"Yes, I believe so. I'll run point on this, and you'll be right next to me. Answer any questions they ask, if you can. You know what you can and cannot say. If they ask something and you're not sure if you should answer, I'll jump in."

"Got it."

"Many of the questions will probably be about the latest victim, and we don't have a lot of answers about her yet. You'll be answering most questions with a 'We're not at liberty to say at this time' or 'We're still waiting on the crime lab to tell us for sure.' Don't worry about it too much. They'll try to push you and sensationalize every little detail. Just don't fall for it. Stay calm, cool, and collected and you'll be fine."

"Okay. Sounds good. See you in five." Wyatt clicked off the cell phone and dropped it into the cup holder in his truck's center console. As he withdrew his hand, he brushed against a manila folder that had been wedged between the seat and the console. The folder was jammed full of paperwork, which now littered the floor of Wyatt's truck. "Arrrrrgh!" growled Wyatt as he guided his truck with one hand and tried to help Jack scoop up the papers with the other. They'd plucked nearly half of the papers from the floorboard when Wyatt's cell phone began to vibrate in the cup holder.

"I've got it," said Jack. "It's probably Duvall again."

"Thanks."

As he pressed the *talk* button, Jack noticed the phone's caller ID flashed PRIVATE NUMBER. "Hello?"

"Ah, this isn't the voice I expected to hear, but this *is* the man I want to talk to," came the sound-modified voice on the other end of the line.

"Listen, Omega! This has to stop! You keep calling us and toying with us, playing these games that you play, and you don't let us join in or give us a fair shake."

Wyatt stopped picking up the papers and stared at Jack in amazement. *How could Omega have found out my private cell phone number?*

"It stops when I say it stops!" roared Omega, clearly annoyed. "I'm calling the shots here, not you. It stops when these people learn their lesson. They know what they have to do. I've told you, and I've told them, and just in case they forget, I leave a note as a reminder. Doesn't seem to be sinking in, though."

"So you help them out a little with that?"

"I'm trying to teach them a lesson. Alas, there are no willing learners out there. Makes me wonder if everyone in this town is totally stupid by birth or by choice."

"Wow, that's rather condescending."

"It is what it is, Detective."

"All right, let me ask you a question. If you're so intent on making people 'face their fears,' then why don't you step out of the shadows and into the light?"

The question caught Omega totally off guard. "Exactly what is it that you think I'm doing? Don't tell me you're dense too, Jack. Don't shatter my image of you."

"Maybe I'm scared of you. Maybe I need to face *my* fears. How do you plan on handling me?"

"Tsk, tsk. Jack, you ought to know me better than that. I *know* your history. I know practically everything there is to know about you. You're not scared of anybody or anything."

"That just proves you're not playing this game fairly."

"How so?"

"Well, you know everything about me, and I've repeatedly asked you questions that you continue to shrug off. I still know *nothing* about you. You didn't strike me as an unfair person in all of this. Maybe I was wrong."

As Omega contemplated his response, Wyatt steered the truck through the side streets and into the back entrance of the police station's parking lot. He grabbed Jack's cell phone and exited the truck to phone Duvall about the latest development. Within seconds, Agent Duvall was running through the parking lot, eyeing Jack's reactions to the dialogue with the killer. Finally, a much-sought-after breakthrough emerged from the conversation—a small tidbit of a bone thrown out by Omega.

"Okay. I'll give you a shot," said Omega. "If I don't like the question, I simply won't answer. You can keep asking until I finally answer one—*and only one*—question. Fair enough?"

"Deal," said Jack, slightly holding his breath. He glanced at Agent Duvall and Chief Hart before blurting out his question. "What is the significance of the omega symbol? We're not sure we get it."

Omega let out a deep breath and began his diatribe. "In the Greek language, omega is the last letter of their alphabet. The last book of the Bible, the book of Revelation, is a preview of a final showdown—the showdown between good and evil. In this 'omega' book, there are twenty-two chapters. The omega chapter is the one I have really taken to heart. The twelfth verse says that Jesus is coming soon, and that He will reward everyone, according to what they've done. Well, there are some people in this town who have done some bad things, and there's not a remorseful bone in their bodies. Not one ounce of regret! No repentance whatsoever. My goal is to correct that error, to get them to face their fears, regardless of whether they happen to be physical, mental, or moral in nature. Some of their fears are imagined, but most of their fears are real. In verse thirteen, it says, 'I am the Alpha and the Omega, the Beginning and the End.' Jesus is the Alpha, the Beginning, the Creator of life. I am His counterpart. They don't seem to be listening to Him, so I 'encourage' them a little. I am the last person they see if they don't turn themselves around. I am the end. The omega, if you will. So you see, I *have* to do this. Jesus compels me to do so. I didn't choose this fate; it chose me."

"You can stop this nonsense!" Jack shouted. "Jesus doesn't tell you to kill people! He wants you to show others how they can change, but you can't do the changing yourself. Christ is the only One in the life-changing business. That's His job, not yours. If you love Him and follow His commands like you say you do, then you'll stop these senseless killings. There are innocent people out here fearing for their lives! Isn't that the exact opposite of what you want? Turn yourself in, Omega. It's the right thing to do. Jesus gave Himself up willingly, so how about you? You'd never be more like Him than giving up your life."

Omega gave the notion a few seconds of thought before he rendered his verdict. "Ya know what? I don't think so. I don't think that's gonna happen. Besides, you asked me *two* questions, and I clearly said you could only ask one. It's about time for a change in scenery anyway. There aren't that many more people in Valley Springs who have a different type of phobia. Maybe I can be like you, Jack. Maybe I can take my 'ministry' to the big city, just like you did. How do you think I'd play in Atlanta? You think I'd make it in the big city, or would I be just another story on the six o'clock news?"

"Honestly, I think you'd be a disappointment," Jack said bluntly.

"Excuse me? A *disappointment?*" Omega screeched. "How so?"

"First of all, it seems to me that you're giving up on Valley Springs. No follow-up on your 'mission.' Sounds to me like you don't finish what you start."

Omega worked hard to calm himself. He seethed at Jack's implication that no one took him or his games seriously, even though that was far from the case. "Tell ya what, Jack. I'm gonna let you go, because it's almost time for you losers to start your press conference, but you remember this. I *will* finish this. I *will* win this game. I always win. Ask my victims if you don't believe me. Oh, that's right. You *can't*! You can't ask them, and you can't save them! I've got a couple more people who need to learn their lesson; then I'm headed to the big city. Atlanta, G-A! Wonder who will get there first, Detective. Me or you? Good-bye for now, Jack. I'll be watching."

Ω 21

The conversation still buzzed through Jack's brain like bumble bees in a flower garden. The press conference was already in full swing, but he was not the star of the show. Agent Duvall and Chief Hart were running point on that, so he wasn't fully focused on his surroundings, and his mind was wandering. All he could think about was that electronically altered voice. Omega. He knew this person or had known others like him at some point in his life. Most of the people he knew from this area were normal, well-adjusted people. Salt-of-the-earth type of folks. But normal was a relative term. Normal compared to what? Charles Manson? Jeffrey Dahmer? The questions gnawed away at his mind as the circus-like atmosphere of the media onslaught continued just over his left shoulder. Which of his friends, former friends, or acquaintances would ever do such a thing? The thought made him numb. He snapped out of his mental digression when he heard another voice—an all-too-familiar voice.

"Chief Hart, what can you tell us about any possible suspects?" Hayden Duvall, guest correspondent with TVBN and twin brother of FBI Agent Hardin Duvall, shouted above the other reporters. In order to avoid any of the ugliness that might have erupted between Chief Hart and his own brother because of their past, Hardin stepped in to answer the question.

"Obviously, we can't get into great detail in an ongoing investigation, but we have identified four or five persons of interest. We've narrowed down the number of suspects considerably, but we've still got some work to do. We're asking the public for patience and calm as we track this guy down. Rest assured, we *will* get him. We want to make sure we bring the right man to justice and that he will be prosecuted to the fullest extent of the law. Next question."

The barrage of voices tumbled over their ears until Hardin pointed at a female reporter near the front.

"What can you tell us about the latest victim? Was the boyfriend involved in any way?" she asked.

"We have interviewed the boyfriend as best as we could under the circumstances. He's obviously very upset about his girlfriend and at the same time trying to get over his own physical trauma—a head injury and a mild concussion. He's not exactly in a condition or state of mind to be interviewed in depth, but we've pretty much ruled him out as a suspect, based on what we were able to get from him," Chief Hart explained.

"But why haven't we seen anyone coming in for an interview or any of you guys going out to question these 'suspects' you say you have?" Hayden said tersely.

"I believe Agent Duvall has answered that, so I won't go into detail over this again. It's still an open investigation, so there are things we just can't say right now."

"It seems to me that either you guys don't have any *viable* suspects, or you haven't discovered any useful evidence at the crime scenes. So is this a case of a professional serial killer outsmarting you or just inept police work?" Hayden retorted.

All eyes shot toward the men on the dais. The members of the press knew that was the death knell of the press conference, and Hardin confirmed it seconds later.

"Sorry about this folks, but we're gonna have to stop right here. Thank you all for attending, and we'll be in touch."

A collective groan swept over the group, yet they continued to shout out their questions to the men. Duvall and Hart scooped up their files and other paperwork and made a rapid exit from the stage, ignoring the reporters completely.

Ω

Omega sat in front of his TV, watching the chaos of the news conference unfold before his eyes. Munching on popcorn and sipping on a soda, he was focused on every word coming from the mouths of the reporters and the police. *A fascinating study of human behavior*, he thought.

He hung on every syllable like a starry-eyed schoolgirl, knowing that he was the reason behind all the hysteria. A warped sense of pride came over him as he reveled in the misfortune he'd caused others. In Omega's warped, sick, and twisted mind he was merely the light that exposed the darkness within the hearts of the townspeople. They had brought this all on themselves. They had not faced their fears, in more ways than one. This town had once been on fire for the Lord. Now it was merely burning, smoldering from within. Smoldering from its lusts, its desires. Omega had lived in Valley Springs all his life, and he'd seen the transformation firsthand. As some of the leaders in the town had aged, no emerging leaders in waiting had assumed the reins. The younger generation had drifted away from the things of God, mainly because they had not been mentored by their elders. They'd *submitted* to their elders, but they'd learned nothing from them. They weren't able to relate to the older generation of saints, so they'd decided to strike out on their own, to search for their own versions of the truth. Sadly, it ended in false hope in the majority of cases. They found comfort in the arms of worldly things. They'd leaned on their own understanding, instead of trusting and living for Jesus. Now they *would* face their fears. Omega would personally see to that. He would spend the rest of this evening planning his next and final lesson for the people of Valley Springs. It would be his most daring, most meaningful lesson to date.

$$\Omega$$

The gang of six had entrenched themselves in the conference room once again, reviewing their responses from the press conference and perusing the short list of people they wanted to bring in for questioning. These people were not officially suspects, but they were persons of interest. Agent Duvall, Chief Hart, and Special Agent Spikes were bouncing ideas off the brains of the other three. Hardin spoke up as the group chatted back and forth.

"Since Omega seems to be forcing our hand, we need to temporarily back off on the idea of interviewing everyone on our lists. We've gotta go with our gut instincts on this. Who are our most obvious suspects, based on motive and opportunity? We need to cherry-pick them from these two groups, simply because the probability of finding Omega is greater if we limit it to these two factors. The odds are in our favor that way."

"Who do we want to bring in?" asked Jack.

"I think each one of us should pick one person, and we'll bring in those six people for an interview. So anyone volunteering to go first?" asked Hardin as he looked at the others seated at the table.

"I'll go," said Dr. Sheffield. "I'll go with a less obvious suspect. Let's bring in the pastor, Noel Marshall."

"Okay, that's one. Who's next?"

Dr. Brown spoke up. "I'll take a more obvious one. I know Dr. Marion Earls has a bad temper, but he's the only ob-gyn in this town. Women here don't have much of a choice when it comes to their health care. He's it. Plus, his rap sheet shows that he's got some priors."

"Let's tweak him a little bit, see what he's made of," said Hardin. "How about you, Martin? Any ideas?"

"I'm going to throw out two people," said Spikes. "You guys tell me what you think. What about the hospital pharmacist or the anesthesiologist? The midazolam is coming from the hospital. Those two must know something."

"Keep both of them. One more name on the list won't hurt. Chief?"

Wyatt cleared his throat, paused for a few seconds, and then held up his index finger. "Let's expound on Agent Spikes's idea. How about someone else within the operating room, someone whom no one else would question."

"Are you suggesting the doctor himself?" Duvall asked.

"Either the surgeon or the charge nurse."

"How many of each do you have?"

"Three surgeons, five charge nurses," said Wyatt.

"Pick the most likely one from each, and we'll have a little chat."

"You got it."

"What do you think, Jack?" Duvall continued.

"My experience and my gut always tell me to go with the one who is least likely to do such a thing, so I'm gonna say … Detective Wayne."

Shocked glances darted from every corner of the room.

"Nick Wayne?" asked Wyatt, clearly puzzled at the choice.

"I didn't say I *believe* he's the guy, but someone's got to pick the person with opportunity. There are some gaps in his timeline that coincide with a couple of the deaths, but I'm not saying by any means that he did it."

Hardin nodded. "No one is above suspicion, Jack. That includes everyone in this room. If that's your choice, we're bringing him in. He's got access to our notes. He's got access to certain areas in the hospital. He's a viable suspect, even though I'm with you in thinking he's probably not our guy."

"Nick's next shift isn't until noon tomorrow," said Chief Hart. "Should we bring him in early or talk to him after his tour?"

"The sooner, the better. Bring him in around 11 a.m. If I'm right, it shouldn't take too long," he said.

"I'll call him," the chief replied.

"All right. One last choice, and then we're setting up interviews as quickly as possible," Hardin concluded.

Agent Duvall leaned forward in his chair, hands folded in front of him like a tepee, and continued with his choice. "This guy's just hit town, but he's had it in for a lot of people, including Chief Hart, Detective Barnhill, and even me." Hardin slowly eyed each member of the group before shocking them all. "We're bringing in Hayden Duvall."

22

Omega sat in stone-cold silence, mentally preparing himself for his next "teaching lesson." Dressed all in black, he could see himself in his mind's eye carrying out the plan to perfection. By his estimation, his lessons were 90 percent mental preparation and planning, and 10 percent action. He'd rehearsed and rehashed the plan a thousand times in his brain. He'd gathered the chloroform, the shoe covers, the black gloves, and other miscellaneous items and tossed them into the black bag. He was most definitely prepared for his moment. Checking his nerves, he held up his right hand. Steady as a rock. Steely nerves were a great asset in his line of work. He'd done enough of these that it had become almost second nature to him. A normal part of his life, like breathing or sleeping. He was as relaxed as one could possibly be.

Omega abruptly rose from his chair and walked over to the refrigerator. Pulling a large glass carafe from the top shelf, he downed several gulps of cold water. He swiped his keys from the kitchen counter and made his way to the SUV parked outside. It was time to go into surveillance mode. He would sit and watch, almost as if he were on a police stakeout. He would wait. And wait. And wait some more. Time was on his side, but on this day, his luck would be excellent—he wouldn't have to wait as long as he originally thought, and his targets were sitting ducks.

$$\Omega$$

"I still don't understand why you guys called me here. Am I a suspect or something?" Pastor Noel Marshall was clearly puzzled. He knew that the police had their hands full with the Omega investigations, so it probably wasn't a social call or a call to ask for his opinion on the case.

Agent Duvall was running the interview and quickly eased Pastor Marshall's misgivings. "No, Pastor. We're just asking some general questions to help us with our investigation, to get the lay of the land, so to speak. We only have three or four questions, and then you'll be on your way, if that's okay with you."

"Yes, sir. That's fine."

"Great. So Pastor, tell me how long you've lived here and how long you've been at your church."

"Well, I was born and reared in Valley Springs. Grew up with both of these boys," Marshall said, gesturing in the direction of Wyatt and Jack. "I've lived here off and on for pretty much all of my life."

"Off and on?" questioned Duvall.

"Aside from pastoring a couple of other churches in neighboring states, those are the only times I can remember not living in Valley Springs."

"Pastor Marshall, tell us about your military service."

The pastor's face drooped and turned pale. A dark cloud seemed to settle over him. He swallowed hard, cleared his throat, and then began to speak. "It's not something I really discuss with a lot of people. Vietnam was a hard time for everyone."

"I understand. Please take as much time as you need."

Pastor Marshall lowered his head and closed his eyes for a few seconds before continuing. "I had originally planned to go to college and study medicine, but my mom had been very ill, so I had to put off my studies for a while. That's when Uncle Sam came knocking at my door. Since I wasn't in school, I *had* to go. I told them about my mom, but my request to stay stateside was denied. I was shipped off to Saigon, so I figured while I was there, I should try to make the best of a bad situation. They put me in as an assistant to the chief medic, kind of letting me learn things on the fly. That was truly a baptism by fire. I saw things there that I never, ever want to see again. Sometimes I still dream about all that stuff. It's hard to even think about it again. But it's also what made me turn my heart toward the things of God. I figured I should finish what I started, so out of a sense of duty, I did the best job I could do in assisting the medic. Truth be told, I could feel myself being called into the ministry even then. Funny how near-death experiences tend to make you draw closer to God."

"Like the old saying goes, 'There are no atheists on a battlefield.' It's sad that it has to come to that to get people right with God. It should be that way every day, regardless of the circumstances," replied Duvall empathetically.

"Amen, Detective. Well said."

"Continue, Pastor."

"Well, I learned everything I could've possibly learned there, but the other men started to notice that I was spending more time ministering to their souls than to their physical injuries. That's when I began to play dual roles as a medical assistant and as a chaplain. My superior officers thought it was a great idea, great for the morale and spiritual health of the other men. Being a sounding board for them mentally, because of some of the things they'd seen, seemed to do them more good than most things I could have done for them in an operating room."

"Thank you for sharing that, Pastor Marshall. I know that was difficult for you. Now let's shift gears a little bit. How often do you go to the hospital on pastoral visitation?"

"At least twice a week. Sometimes three times, depending on who's sick or having surgery."

"So you know your way around the hospital. You know what's going on with each patient."

"Yes, sir. I'd have to say I know almost everyone there."

"You know their disease or condition and how to medically treat them?"

"Yes, but I'm no doctor. I would never give advice or even be expected to give any to the doctors and nurses down there. But I know why they do what they do and how serious the situation is, based on the treatment."

"You mean with pharmaceuticals?"

"I suppose. Drugs. Physical therapy. Rehab. Whatever is necessary to remedy the situation."

Agent Duvall pushed back from the table and stood, extending his hand to Pastor Marshall. "We're sorry for the inconvenience, Pastor. Thank you for coming in on such short notice. If we have any other questions, we'll give you a call."

"My pleasure. I hope I was of some help to your case. Maybe I'm not a suspect anymore," he said as a sly grin etched its way across his face.

"No, your information was very helpful. Thanks again for coming in."

As Pastor Marshall made his way toward the exit, Agent Spikes, Chief Hart, and Officer Barnhill rounded the doorway of the interrogation room where Duvall had just conducted the interview. The others had been watching their conversation from behind a two-way mirror, checking for certain facial expressions, body language, or inconsistencies in his story. The verdict was unanimous.

"He's clean," remarked Agent Spikes.

"No way he did it," added Barnhill.

"I don't think so either," chipped in Chief Hart.

"I'll make it a consensus. You guys know him better than I do, but if he did it, he's got four law enforcement officials totally fooled, and someone ought to hand him the award for best actor right now," uttered Duvall. "Okay, then. Let's strike him off the suspect list."

"So, who's next?" asked Agent Spikes.

$$\Omega$$

Omega steered his SUV into a forested area near his next target's home. He parked the vehicle on a small dirt path and silently pushed open the driver's side door. The ticking of the SUV's cooling engine was the only sound he could hear. Exiting the vehicle, he shuffled his feet a few yards away into the nearby underbrush. He grabbed several downed branches and dead tree limbs left over from a previous thunderstorm and camouflaged his black SUV. He had done this so many times that he'd become a master at the craft. From the highway and from the target's home, he had become virtually invisible in the dense undergrowth. Satisfied that the SUV couldn't be seen by anyone, Omega reentered the vehicle and settled in for the long haul. He had a bottle of water and several nonperishable items to snack on, in case he needed a quick burst of energy. As he nestled into the bucket seat, he checked his watch and then produced a pair of binoculars and a pistol. For now, he would watch the home for any signs of activity. In just a few short hours, the time would be right for action, regardless of who was inside the house. Omega would be ready.

23

"Deputy Wayne is on security detail right now, but he should be getting off in about an hour and a half." Chief Hart spat out the information, although he felt a bit uneasy about the interrogation of one of his own. He knew that if anything was amiss, it would reflect on him personally and on his whole department in general.

"Radio him and ask him if he can have a sit-down after his shift is over. Don't make a huge deal out of it. Tell him it's routine-type stuff. I'll have Detective Barnhill sit in on the interview with me, just for everyone's peace of mind and so Nick won't feel as if he's being grilled like some ordinary perp," Agent Duvall responded.

"I'm on it," Wyatt sighed.

"Let's use these next forty-five minutes or so to collect our thoughts, take a break, grab something to eat, or make some phone calls—whatever you feel like you need to do to get away from this case for a short while. Let's refresh our brains, and we'll meet back here in forty-five."

$$\Omega$$

Omega had watched the home like a hawk, waiting for the slightest motion from inside, the smallest opening so that he could pounce. Several hours passed before he picked up on an unguarded movement, a movement unlike the gentle back-and-forth swaying of the pine trees or the occasional shedding of their needles. Someone was coming outside. It was just the man Omega was hoping to see. Quietly, he slipped out of the SUV, grabbing the firearm as he went. He left the driver's side door ajar and crouched down beside one of the tires. Digging into his shirt pocket, he produced a handful of rubber bullets and chambered them. Omega rose slowly, using the hood of the SUV to steady his shot. He would wait until the man moved the walkie-talkie away from his right ear before he fired.

Ω

"Nick, we need to talk to you tonight at the end of your shift. It's nothing major, just some loose ends we need to tie up. Can you make that happen?" Wyatt asked.

"Not a problem, Chief. I've got just a little over an hour until my replacement comes in. I think he's one of Agent Spikes's guys from the GBI, so when he gets here I'll head into the station house."

"Thanks. We'll get you in and out as quickly as we can."

"See you then."

"Ten-four. Out."

"Ten-four."

Officer Wayne clipped the walkie-talkie to his belt and then stepped forward to the edge of the porch.

Ω

Omega made one last check of his firearm. *Silencer secured. Safety off. Sight and scope picture-perfect straight.* He raised the gun, keeping it balanced in his hands by the hood of his SUV. He watched as Officer Wayne clipped the radio to his belt and walked toward the end of the home's front porch—right into the crosshairs of Omega's gun.

Ω

The rubber bullet made a tiny *cra-a-ack* as it hurtled from the gun's barrel in the direction of Officer Wayne. It struck him in the right temple, just above the ear, with the force of five sledgehammers. The blow caused him to black out temporarily, losing all sense of coordination and awareness. He fell forward, face first, like a tree freshly cut by a lumberjack. Officer Wayne's body produced a muffled thud as he tumbled the three feet down to the soft earth below the porch, sending up a small cloud of dust as he landed. Luckily for him, his forehead hit the ground first, leaving him with only a nasty, bloody gash instead of a crushed face. However, the combination of the gunshot and the fall would put him out of commission for a while, leaving him knocked out and bleeding on the front lawn. Omega watched through the scope, proud of his extremely accurate aim. He continued to search for signs of movement from inside the house, as well as any stirring from the unconscious man on the ground. Five minutes of no motion prompted Omega to make his move. He slung a black bag, filled with everything he would need, over his shoulder and crept toward the house. Pausing briefly at the edge of the lawn, he could see the side of the man's head where the rubber bullet had stamped its imprint. The spot near his temple was bright crimson and already starting to swell as a nice welt made its appearance. The blood from the cut on his forehead trickled across his face like a small stream and pooled between his cheek and the ground. The gash wasn't big enough for Officer Wayne to bleed out, so Omega didn't worry too much about him. The man would live, with maybe a small scar as a souvenir to show for it. He stepped over the prone body and slithered toward the house, stopping to take cover at the edge of the front porch. He slid the bag from his shoulder and set the next part of his plan into motion.

$$\Omega$$

"I just talked to Officer Wayne. He's going to stop by after his shift," Chief Hart said as he passed Agent Duvall in the corridor.

"Great. We need him eliminated as a suspect as soon as we can. That'll be one less thing to worry about."

"Right. That's for sure."

"Excuse me, Chief," Duvall said, pointing to the caller ID on his chirping cell phone. "I need to take this." Duvall ducked into a side office and shut the door behind him, his face etched with a clearly annoyed look. He clicked the *talk* button and snapped, "Kinda busy here, Hayden. What do you need?"

"I know, I know. But I've got something here that may be of interest to you and your case."

Just like Hayden to over-dramatize everything, Hardin thought. *Why does he insist on playing these games? Why doesn't he just tell me?* "All right, Hayden. Make it quick, okay? Spit it out."

"We've got a copy of the surveillance tape from the pharmacy."

"And?"

"There are a couple of people back there who we don't recognize. They're almost purposely staying out of camera range."

"I think the TV lights are frying your brain, Hayden. Why would someone who works there stay out of the camera's view on purpose? That makes no sense at all."

"Maybe because the person *doesn't* work there. Or maybe the person isn't *supposed* to be back there."

The thought stopped Agent Duvall cold. Leave it to his twin brother to show him another angle he'd somehow missed. "So how is the guy getting back there? The pharmacy has restricted access. Key-card swipes. Sign-in sheets."

"It's gotta be someone the rest of the pharmacy staff knows. Whoever it is pretty much has unfettered access, whether he has his own key-card or someone's letting him in," replied Hayden.

"Plus, you've gotta figure they trust him enough to have access, yet no one in the pharmacy seems to notice when bottle after bottle of midazolam goes missing," Agent Duvall conjectured.

"Right. Now here's the question I'm asking. How much of this can we run with on TVBN? I want to be able to cover this as best as I can without jeopardizing your case."

"You can show the tape in its entirety. Seems to be pretty bland stuff.

But please do *not* speculate on anyone within the pharmacy just yet. Point the conversation in the direction of missing drugs, not the person who might be actually taking them. We clear on that?"

"Crystal. Just make sure we get the breaking news first when you catch this guy. Exclusives. Live one-on-one interviews. The whole nine yards."

"I promise. Done deal, brother. Thank you. There *is* a heart beating inside that chest of yours."

"Just trying to look out for you, even if we sometimes don't see eye to eye," Hayden said. "So, what's next? Where do you guys go from here?"

"We've got a person of interest coming in for an interview pretty soon, and now I'm going to have to send Agent Spikes or some of the other GBI boys down to the pharmacy. We need to cross-reference the key-card swipes with the sign-in sheets to see if there are names that aren't showing up on both lists. If we find the person who isn't flagged on both lists, then we may uncover the identity of our killer."

Ω

Omega inched his way onto the wrap-around porch from the front, gradually working his way to the back door of the house. Peeking in through the small window next to the breakfast nook, he saw the objects of his next lesson sitting on the couch with their backs to him. They were watching television, seemingly locked in visually and emotionally. Perfect. These two would be easy pickings. Omega's heart raced as he focused on the task at hand: the impending abduction of Heather Barnhill and Annette Hart.

Ω24

They had left the back door unlocked. They knew they weren't supposed to, especially with a serial killer still uncaptured in their town. But why should Annette Hart and Heather Barnhill worry for their safety? They were under twenty-four hour surveillance. Local police officers or GBI agents were standing guard right outside the house. What if the men needed to come inside for something, like a glass of water or to use the restroom? It was easier to leave the door unlocked so that they wouldn't have to answer the door each time. The officers could just come and go as they pleased. A few officers voiced their objections over this open-door policy but to no avail. As it turned out, the officers had good reason to be concerned.

Omega ducked low as he edged away from the window. He pulled out the firearm once more and then quietly slipped the black bag over his shoulder. Adjusting the black glove on his left hand, he took one last deep breath and twisted the doorknob. The lock clicked as he silently pushed the door inward. Neither woman turned around, their eyes still glued to the talk show playing on the television. Besides, they were so used to lawmen traipsing in and out of the house that they never turned around anymore when the door opened. Omega crept forward a few feet and then dropped to one knee, extending the gun toward the woman on the right side of the couch. He fired—and the rubber bullet thumped against the skull of Annette Hart, rendering her instantly unconscious. Before Heather Barnhill could register that something had happened to Annette, Omega had taken a half-step to his left and shot past the slumped-over Annette. The beginnings of a scream escaped Heather's throat, but then the bullet crashed into her right temple, in almost the exact spot where a bullet had struck Officer Wayne. She groaned softly before she too passed out. Omega leapt to his feet and studied his handiwork. Two shots; two take-downs. *Quite the marksman*, he gloated to himself. Annette's body leaned against the right arm of the couch, her head tilted back at an awkward angle. Heather had pitched forward and fallen off the sofa. She lay on her left side, facing the couch, a huge welt already forming between her right eye and ear. Pausing only for a few seconds, Omega sprang to his work. The women offered no resistance as he pulled their wrists behind them. Grabbing a strand of nylon rope from his bag, he wound it around Annette's wrists first and then Heather's. He checked once more to see if they were still unconscious. *Still out. Great!* he thought as he dug into the bag and produced two black hoods. He draped the hoods over the women's heads and then grabbed an index card, which he taped carefully to the television. Finally, he pulled a set of handcuffs from the black bag and looped one side through the rope that connected the two women. He would use this as a makeshift leash when the women came to, but for now, he was their primary means of transportation. Omega propped both women up against the back of the couch, stuck his head between them, and hoisted both women simultaneously over his shoulders. He lumbered sideways through the still-open door, briefly stopping to look both ways to make sure that the coast was clear. Convinced there was no one else around, he hurried across the porch, down the steps, and out to the SUV. He clicked open the hatch with his key remote and then dumped both of the women in with a loud thump. He took a small rag, doused it with chloroform, and held it up to their noses for a few seconds, just for good measure and for his own reassurance that they would be knocked out for a long while. One shot of midazolam for each sealed the deal. He dropped the rag and the syringes into his black bag, stripped off his gloves and shoe covers, and climbed into the cab. A wicked grin crossed his face, a smile that signified a plan carried out to perfection. Mission accomplished.

$$\Omega$$

The GBI agent arrived just a few minutes late for his scheduled shift at guarding the Hart home—he'd stopped at a convenience store for coffee.

When he arrived at the house and saw Officer Wayne crumpled on the front lawn, he snapped up the microphone of his radio, sending his hot cup of coffee skittering across the floorboard of the passenger side. He cursed but immediately called for backup as he sprinted toward the body.

"This is Agent Locke of the GBI. We have a man down! I repeat: we have a man down! He is unconscious but still breathing. Appears to have a blunt-force trauma wound to the head. Send a bus—and hurry!"

Agent Spikes keyed the microphone and helped clarify the situation. "Ten-four, Agent Locke. Bus is on its way. We have backup on its way as well. Proceed with extreme caution and secure the premises. We need to make sure that the women are safe."

"Ten-four," Locke whispered.

Inside the station house, Agent Spikes yelled down the hallway to anyone on the team within earshot. "Hardin! Wyatt! Jack! It's Officer Wayne! He's down!"

Chief Hart was the first one through the doorway, followed closely by Hardin and Jack.

"What do you mean, he's down?" shouted a wide-eyed Hart as he jogged down the hall.

"One of my guys found him. He's alive, but he appears to have a blunt-force trauma injury to his head."

"The girls!" Hart exclaimed. "Heather and Annette!"

"You boys get over there!" ordered Agent Duvall. "Agent Spikes and I will be over as soon as we can. Go! Go! Go!"

Wyatt and Jack grabbed a set of keys for one of the police cruisers and raced for the parking lot. Wyatt hurriedly cranked the car, rammed it into gear, and squealed his tires as he tore into the street. Neither he nor Jack was thinking clearly as they ripped through town. They'd flipped on the red and blue flashing lights but neglected to turn on the siren. Both men were silent as they darted toward the Harts' home, each one thinking about his wife. Each one praying that this monster hadn't gotten to them first. But neither of their wives had ever been diagnosed with any type of phobia, had they?

Wyatt finally broke the silence. "We need to try their cell phones," he blurted.

"I'll check Heather's first," Jack answered, already beginning to punch in the phone number. Four rings. No answer. "What's Annette's number?" Wyatt recited the phone number as Jack dialed it in. One ring; then it went directly to her voicemail. "No answer on either one."

Wyatt slammed his fist on the dashboard and sped up. His mind raced nearly as fast as the police car. He was truly worried now for the women's safety. "I know this is personal stuff, but has Heather ever been diagnosed with any kind of anxiety disorder?"

"No," replied Jack. "How about Annette?"

"Never, but ..." Wyatt hesitated.

"But what?"

"Most people have some kind of fear, some anxiety that eats at their very core, even if it's not diagnosed by a doctor. I think Annette would fit into that category. Heck, *I* would fit into that category."

"Heather would fall into that same type of category, and I just might as well. But let's not get ahead of ourselves. They may be okay. Maybe we simply can't get in touch with them. Bottom line is, we don't need to panic just yet. We won't know until we get there."

"Hold on," said Wyatt. "We're about to find out."

The car almost slid on two wheels as it cut the corner of the gravel driveway just off Highway 28. The tires slung rocks that pinged beneath the undercarriage of the vehicle, but Wyatt didn't seem to care. His eyes were focused on the road ahead and all the law enforcement vehicles parked near his home. He'd barely put the car into parking gear before he and Jack leapt out. As they raced up the walkway leading to his home, Wyatt shot a glance to his left and saw the EMS crew tending to a dazed Nick Wayne. He held up a finger to one of the paramedics, indicating to him that he would be back to check on Officer Wayne very shortly. The men approached Wyatt's front door and were met by a small army of law enforcement officers. The look on each man's face seemed to say it all before Chief Hart could even get the question out of his mouth. "Somebody talk to me!" he shouted.

Ω 25

Agent Locke heard the shout as he stood inside the house and dashed outside to meet Chief Hart and Detective Barnhill. He quickly ushered them into the home, where he proceeded to explain what they'd discovered so far.

"Guys, I'm sorry to be the one to have to do this, but here's what we've got. It's definitely our man. He apparently took out Officer Wayne with rubber bullets. Ambushed him—"

"Rubber bullets?" Jack interrupted.

"Apparently he wanted to knock him out, not kill him. Either that, or—"

"Or he wasn't the one Omega wanted," blurted Wyatt.

"Heather and Annette?" a clearly irritated Jack asked. The agent's downcast eyes told them everything his lips did not. The two women were gone. "We've got no signs of forced entry, no signs of a struggle, and no blood anywhere. CSU is combing for fibers, hair, or anything else of note. Right now, we've gotta go on the assumption that he's got them."

Jack dropped his head into his hands in helplessness, while Wyatt stomped back outside, desperately trying to regain his composure. As his mind imploded with all of the possible scenarios of how this could end, he caught a glimpse of Officer Wayne being loaded into a waiting ambulance. Wyatt made a beeline to the EMS vehicle and stuck his head around the door. The medical personnel were securing the gurney holding a still-stunned Wayne when one of them noticed Hart and spoke up.

"Looks like he'll be okay. Some contusions, welts, and lacerations, along with a mild concussion. He'll live, but he'll need some rest."

"Okay. Thanks for the update."

Officer Wayne came to, just long enough to mutter a few words to his chief. "Annette … Mrs. Barnhill … it's … it's my fault."

"Nonsense, Officer," Wyatt reassured him. "You were ambushed. There was nothing you could have done that would have made any difference. Don't worry about that right now. We'll get him, and we'll get the girls back." Wyatt squeezed Nick's foot, but the pained expression never left his deputy's face. Whether it was pain or guilt or a combination of both, Wyatt couldn't tell. As the ambulance rolled away, he put his hands on his hips and exhaled heavily. So many emotions welled up inside of him—anger and confusion and helplessness, all rolled into one gigantic outburst, waiting to boil to the surface. He wasn't even sure he believed his own statement about finding the women. It was one thing when the victim was someone else. Now, his wife and her friend were the victims. He knew the likelihood of finding them alive was miniscule at best, but he refused to acknowledge that possibility. He would not believe it. It couldn't happen here, not in their own home—not in Valley Springs. Yet the stark reality of it all was staring them all in the face. Maybe this town was like the rest of the world, with all the vices and depravities. The peace and isolation Valley Springs had once enjoyed was now being wiped away like chalk from a blackboard, leaving smudges in their lives that might never be erased.

Wyatt shook himself and focused his mind on the task at hand. Someone had to find Annette and Heather, and he would be the one to do it. He marched back toward his house, walking in on a conversation between Agent Locke and Jack. Jack was doing his level best to hold it together, but the redness of his eyes and the tearstains on his cheeks gave him away.

"We're thinking it's been less than thirty minutes, so we're watching the highways in and out of here," Locke said. "The trail is still very warm, so we need to move now."

"What do you need me to do?" asked Jack.

The agent turned to Wyatt and Jack, phrasing his next statement as carefully as he possibly could. "Guys, I don't have the authority to make that call, but both of you have been in this game long enough to know that you need to take yourselves off this case. It's too emotional, too personal, and too close to home. At the same time, I wouldn't dare take either of you off the case because it *is* personal. It only makes you even more focused, in my opinion. You guys are too experienced and too good at what you do. To *not* have you on the case would be to hamper the case."

"Thanks. If CSU finds anything, will you let us know?" Jack had no sooner finished his sentence than Wyatt's phone began to chirp.

Wyatt checked the caller ID. It was Hardin. "You got anything?" Chief Hart asked rather abruptly as he put the call on speaker.

"Not yet, but I need you guys to stay put. Agent Spikes and I are on our way. We're gonna examine every last speck of dust, if that's what it takes to catch this animal. How are you and Jack holding up?"

"Pretty well, considering the circumstances. We haven't choked anyone yet, and we haven't totally dissolved into a puddle of tears."

"When I get there, I'm pulling you two to the side, and we're gonna pray. This case won't get solved without God's help, and right now, I think you both could use a comforting touch. Plus, it'll get us all focused."

Immediately, Hardin's words sent a wave of peace rippling through the hearts and minds of both men. It was as if the open wound of their pain had been healed, if only for a short time. Sure, the pain and uncertainty was still there, but their perspective shifted and was clarified. They knew they had a job to do, and they would do it to the best of their abilities—Annette's and Heather's lives depended on them. Deep down inside, however, the men knew that the Lord held the two women in the palm of His hand—a sliver of comfort in the midst of the melee that swirled around them. At once, the atmosphere around them changed, and both Jack and Wyatt seemed to sense it. As the Lord's peace slowly began to wash over both of them, they saw Agent Duvall's vehicle pull up to the home. The agents sprang from the car, Duvall pointing his passenger, Agent Spikes, to the house to oversee the ongoing investigation. Hardin led Wyatt and Jack over to a secluded spot on the property, where the three of them spent ten-minutes in private, shedding tears and pleading for the Lord's help. Once the three men had composed themselves, they strode purposefully up the gravel drive toward the crime scene.

As they ducked under the yellow crime scene tape and trudged up the hill, Agent Duvall whispered, "You guys know I should take you both off this case because of protocol with family members and such, but I'm not going to do it. I prefer to give you the benefit of the doubt and let common sense prevail. However, when we get close enough to name a suspect or bring him down, both you guys are going to have to disappear. I worry about your emotions boiling to the surface. You don't want to do anything stupid to ruin your careers. We also don't want to give the defense lawyers anything to hang their hats on when it comes time to go to trial. They'd say the perp was framed, that it was a conflict of interest with you two working your wives' case. I'd just rather not go there, and the district attorney would rather not go there either. You okay with that? Am I making myself clear?"

"I understand," said Wyatt.

"Got it. No problem," Jack replied.

Once inside the house, Agent Locke debriefed everyone who had recently arrived on the scene and then handed the reins of the case over to Agent Duvall. The law enforcement officers present at the crime scene were put through their paces once again, double-checking what they'd previously done. Right in the midst of the process, the agent's cell phone started to buzz. He glanced down at the caller ID. *Dr. London Brown.*

"Yes, Dr. Brown. Do you have anything for me?" Hardin asked.

"Yes, sir. Someone slipped a DVD under the windshield wiper of one of our squad cars. The envelope has your name on the front, so Dr. Sheffield and I have yet to look at it. It's also got a number written just below your name, with the words 'You'll find this interesting' right underneath the number."

"What kind of number?" Hardin demanded.

"It looks like a counter number. A certain place on the DVD that this person wants you to see."

Hardin suddenly recalled the conversation he'd had with his brother concerning a pharmacy surveillance tape a couple of hours earlier. *Hayden's really outdone himself this time,* Hardin thought. *He's helping our case without drawing any extra attention to himself or our relationship. He's sincerely trying to keep this under wraps.*

"Okay. Open it, cue it up to that time, and then pause the DVD. We're on our way back. They're still processing the scene here, so there's not much else I can do. I'm bringing Chief Hart and Officer Barnhill with me. They need to be away from here." Hardin disconnected the line and whispered to a couple of agents that he had pressing business back at the police station. He marched outside and found Wyatt and Jack near the spot where they'd found Nick Wayne.

"Wyatt and Jack, come with me!" he exclaimed urgently.

Chief Hart's brow furrowed with concern. "What is it? What's happening?"

"Someone's left us an anonymous tip back at the station house. This may be the big break that we need!"

The three men scrambled into the agent's car and roared away.

26

The men rode in silence, with nothing but the sound of tires humming across asphalt at a high rate of speed. The anticipation of what Dr. Brown had found set their senses on edge, increasingly more so since being pulled away from an active crime scene, especially one involving Annette Hart and Heather Barnhill.

There better be something of utmost urgency on that DVD, Hardin thought, *or I'm gonna be beyond ticked. It's gotta be nothing less than the key to unlocking these cases.*

Jack and Wyatt were a bundle of nerves, emotionally torn in the cruelest possible way. Both wanted to be back at the crime scene, around familiar surrounding and first to know if any news broke. At the same time, they were bound by their duties as law enforcement officers to do their job to the best of their ability, no matter who the victims happened to be. The challenge for Jack and Wyatt at this point was to stay poised and keep focused.

The intensity of the day had seeped its way into the very core of the three men, so it was no surprise when Hardin, Wyatt, and Jack jumped at the sound of the cell phone ring that shattered their silence. It was Jack's phone this time.

"Detective Barnhill," he answered from speaker mode.

"Well, if it isn't my old friend Jack. A voice from my past. *Our* past."

Omega! "Where's my wife, you—"

"Ah-ah, Jack. Patience, my friend. Patience."

Wyatt and Hardin snapped to attention, as they could hear the voice on the other end of the line. The conversation continued.

"I'm not your friend right now," Jack said, trying to remain calm. "I want to know where you've taken our wives!"

"Well, if you guys are as smart as you claim to be, you'll find them soon enough, but first things first. How's Officer Wayne doing?" asked Omega.

"He'll live. You bloodied him up pretty good."

"Excellent. He wasn't the target anyway. He just happened to be in the way—the wrong place at the wrong time. Collateral damage, so to speak."

"So our wives were your target?" assumed Jack.

"I had to get your attention somehow."

"Are they okay?"

"Yes, they're fine. They're resting. Now stop interrupting me, so I can get a word in edgewise!" huffed Omega impatiently.

"What did they ever do to you? They don't fit your way of doing things. They've never been diagnosed with any kind of phobia or anxiety disorder," pushed Jack as he glanced at the others in the car.

"Technically, no. Like I said, I had to get your attention somehow. Besides, I think you and Hart underestimate your spouses. They have phobias—phobias that almost everyone has that are undiagnosed."

"So now everyone has a phobia of some kind?"

"Not everyone, Jack. Some people live their lives free of fear. Those are the people who totally put their trust in Jesus. I'm simply trying to get them to flesh that out, to live out what they *say* they believe."

"By scaring them to death?" Jack protested.

"No, by making them face their fears. And as you can see, I've saved the best for last. Jack and Heather. Wyatt and Annette. You say that you have no fears, Jack. I'm putting that statement to the test right now, for you and for Wyatt. What will you two do, if or when your spouses disappear? Are you scared? Anxious? Aren't you concerned at all, Jack?"

"Of course I am," Jack hoarsely whispered.

"Then you're a hypocrite, because you said you had no fears at all.

Don't you trust Jesus to take care of your precious Heather?" asked Omega.

"I trust Jesus. It's *you* I don't trust."

"Aw-w-w, Jack. You hurt my itty-bitty feelings! Now, is it safe to say that you and Wyatt, brave and fearless lawmen as you claim to be, have a phobia that you possibly didn't know you had?" There were several seconds of silence before Omega continued. "I'll take your silence as a yes. You know it's true, and it's true for your wives as well. In fact, you and Wyatt may have more than one phobia."

"Really, now! How so?"

"Fear of failure kinda creeps up on you two sometimes, doesn't it? Failure to stop Hinckley in Washington, and now the possibility of not finding your wives. It's all a bit much for you, eating at your gut like—"

"We don't dwell on Washington," Jack broke in. "And we *will* find them."

"I wish you would stop interrupting me! How rude of you! Didn't your mama teach you any manners? You talk mighty big for someone in your position. The clock is ticking, Jack. Time is running out. Are you up to it, or is the fear of being a failure again overwhelming you?" Omega interrogated.

"Let me tell you something, Omega. You can point out a person's human side all you like. His fears. His failures. The down side of your philosophical argument is that no matter how much you try to goad someone, you can't willingly *make* that person conquer his fears. You don't get to decide who faces their fears and who doesn't. That's God's call, and God certainly doesn't need your help. Sounds to me like you have control issues—either that or a God complex. This utopian perfection seems to be something you'd like to have, but it doesn't seem to be working out too well for you, does it? Maybe that's a fear *you* need to face."

"Enough!" screamed Omega. "I am in charge here, so you better listen! I've already told you that I'm taking my act to Atlanta, so if you want any chance of saving your wives before I leave, I'd keep my pie hole shut if I were you."

"Oh, so *now* you're going to give us a sporting chance of saving Heather and Annette? How noble of you. You're finally gonna let us play your little game. I keep telling everyone you're a nice guy; you're just misunderstood," said Jack, almost mockingly.

"Sarcasm is the sincerest form of flattery, Detective Barnhill."

"Glad you like it. Now where's my wife?"

"They're sleeping, but I'll give them a shot of epinephrine to wake them up. All in due time, Jack. All in due time. Here's what you need to remember. The only thing that might be able to save your wife and the wife of our dear friend Wyatt, short of their actually facing their fears, is one simple word. A word that describes a phobia that most of us have, but virtually no one bothers to diagnose. There's usually no need to diagnose it, but in your case there is. Let's see how smart you are, Jack. Can you catch me? I'm about to disappear. Tick tock!"

"What's the word?" Jack shouted into the phone.

"Taphophobia," Omega whispered.

"What? Say that again!"

"You heard me. I'm not repeating myself. Figure this one out for yourself, but you better hurry. Lives are depending on you. See you soon, maybe even in Atlanta, Jack. Hugs and kisses to Hardin and Wyatt."

Jack heard the *click* of the call disconnecting. "Hello? Hello?" He shut off the phone and turned to the other men, who were staring wide-eyed at him. "He said the only thing that could save Heather and Annette was the word *taphophobia*," said Jack.

"Taphophobia? What does that mean?" asked Wyatt.

"I don't know, but we'll ask Dr. Brown. He should know."

"We'll ask him before we take a look at the DVD. It may give us more insight as to what we're looking for," Agent Duvall suggested. "Hold on, boys. We're about to find out soon enough." Duvall slung the car around the corner without so much as tapping his brakes. The car's wheels hugged the road but sent out a small squeal in protest as they made the turn leading to the station house. They were only two blocks away, but it seemed like a thousand miles. Time appeared to stand still, despite the speed at which Duvall was driving. The car screeched through the parking lot, barely missing several police cruisers. No sooner than Hardin had switched off the ignition and removed the keys than Jack and Wyatt ripped off their seatbelts and bolted for the conference room; Agent Duvall trailed not too far behind them. Huffing and puffing, the trio slid into the conference room where Dr. Brown had the DVD player cued up and ready to go.

"Whenever you're ready, gentlemen," Dr. Brown said quietly, clearly noticing their frazzled urgency.

"Hit it," ordered Hardin, jabbing a finger at the DVD player as Wyatt spoke up.

"London, we've got a quick question. Omega just called Jack's cell phone, and he may have given us a clue. What does the term *taphophobia* mean? The fear of what?"

Dr. Brown's eyes almost leapt from their sockets at Chief Hart's question. His reply unnerved everyone in the room. "Oh, my God! We've got to hurry!"

Ω 27

"What is it? What does it mean?" bellowed Jack.

Dr. Brown had already pressed the play button on the DVD, and the surveillance pictures soundlessly rolling across the screen. His eyes shot from the men to the television and then back to the men. "Taphophobia is the fear of being buried alive!"

The mental images of what that implied or what that might entail sent shudders through their very souls. It was so gruesome, so unthinkable that none of them were able to dwell on it for very long. Instead, they followed the cue of Agent Duvall, who turned his eyes toward the TV screen. They all knew what was at stake. There was no need to verbalize it again.

"What are we looking at here, Dr. Brown?" Hardin asked, breaking the silent tension that had crept its way into the room.

"This is the central security camera from inside the hospital pharmacy. We've identified most of the personnel and interviewed them at length, but there's one person—one set of shoes that the camera catches—that we can't seem to figure out who it is. This guy is purposely staying out of camera range. He knows where they are and avoids them."

"So what does that mean?" Jack said, a hint of annoyance in his voice.

"It means that this mystery person might be our guy. He's got access to the pharmacy, which means he's got access to the midazolam and the epinephrine. He's dancing around the camera like he's some kind of Baryshnikov."

"The disc is time- and date-stamped, so why don't we just bring in someone who we've already identified as being in the pharmacy at that particular time, and …"

Jack's voice trailed off as suddenly, the image smacked them all in the face like a bucket of ice water. The big break they needed was making its presence known. The screen showed an image of a syringe falling from the grasp of an unidentified man. As he attempted to catch it before it clattered to the ground, another carton dropped from his fingers and landed on the pharmacy floor. The box was square and appeared to contain a multidose vial of liquid.

Dr. Brown almost jumped out of his seat. "I'd know that box anywhere! That's epinephrine! And I can't be sure, but that syringe looks like a midazolam syringe. A lot of drugs come packaged like that, but I'd be willing to bet that it's midazolam. I *know* that square box is epinephrine. I know that for a fact."

"So what makes this special?" Hardin spat. "You can't tie it to anything. All it does is prove that Omega uses these two drugs. We already knew that!"

Duvall got his answer two seconds later. The man's face slowly appeared in the camera's lens, like a zeppelin across a clear blue sky. The man bent at the waist, scooped up the vial and the syringe, and shoved them into his pocket.

"Stop! Back that up a couple of frames!" Wyatt ordered.

Dr. Brown snatched up the remote and rewound the image in slow-motion mode. He pressed the frame-advance button, which made the video proceed one image at a time. Then they all saw it. As the man reached down to pluck the syringe from the floor, he twisted his head slightly, tilting it toward the camera and giving them a profile view of his face. Omega had slipped up.

"Whoa! Right there!" Agent Duvall shouted as he pointed at the television screen.

The man was a well-dressed gentleman, appearing to be in his late fifties or early sixties, graying a little around the temples, and somewhat muscular for someone his age.

Wyatt tore from his chair so violently that it flipped over backward and bounced off the floor with a thump. "Let's go! I know who that is!"

"I do, too!" shouted Dr. Brown. "That's—"

"I know! I know! London, stay here!" Wyatt ordered. "Call for backup at Klayman Funeral Home!"

Wyatt, Jack, and Hardin stormed the door, only Wyatt knowing exactly where they were heading.

Ω

Omega disconnected the voice modification system, slapped his cell phone shut, and shoved it into his pocket. A few more chores to do, and then he would begin the research. Atlanta was a big city with millions of people. For Omega, it was a veritable gold mine of hypocrites who needed to face the truth of who they truly were, down in the depths of their soul—people who had the knowledge but not the heart. He would be the one to show them. He would make them face their fears. It was for their own good, he reasoned. With such a sprawling metropolis to cover, he would need to have a plan to attack it strategically. It would be a challenge, to be sure, but one he relished greatly. For now, he had two smaller problems to attend to before he could direct all of his attention toward Atlanta. Their names were Heather and Annette.

Still bound together by the nylon rope and the handcuffs, the women lay on their sides, back to back, in the back of Omega's black SUV. They continued to be in a steady state of unconsciousness. Omega brought the vehicle to a stop at the rear entrance of his place of employment, a business that he had owned for quite a while. He'd inherited it from his dad, who'd inherited it from his father-in-law. Family-owned and operated for decades. Business was always booming, even in a town as small as Valley Springs. Lately, business was more than booming; it was exploding. He'd personally seen to that.

Omega bolted inside and snatched a second set of keys from his desk. Briskly moving back outside, he unlocked the doors to the hearse, which was parked under an aluminum shelter to keep it out of the hot, southern Georgia sun. He fired the engine and cranked up the air-conditioning to its maximum level. Waiting inside the rear door was a new casket he had placed there the previous night. The casket was very heavy even without a body inside, and it had taken almost every ounce of his strength to load the casket onto the cart. Now, the rest of his task was a breeze—he slid it from the cart into the hearse and then flipped up both the lower and upper halves of the casket's lid. Crawling back out of the hearse, he popped the back hatch of the SUV, yanked the women up by the handcuffs, and heaved their dead weight into the casket. Omega snatched the black hoods from their heads and adjusted their bodies into a better position within the casket—his perfectionist nature was showing. The women still were on their sides, so that both of them would fit inside. Once he'd adjusted their hands and feet, smoothed their hair, and shut the casket lid, he eased into the driver's seat of the hearse and headed for Pine Knoll Cemetery. He was pleased with himself and smiled as he pondered what he'd accomplished. In his mind, it was a job well done.

$$\Omega$$

The Bureau-issued vehicle ripped down the narrow streets of Valley Springs in the direction of Klayman Funeral Home. They'd taken several corners on two wheels, but no one inside the car seemed to notice. They were singularly focused on one thing: the capture of Omega. The car swung around a curve and then made a hard left, heading north on Honeysuckle Lane. They took another left on Cobblestone Drive and a quick right onto Willow Street, jokingly nicknamed "Widow Street" because it was the street where the funeral home was located. The car bounced over the bulge in the asphalt, where a drainage pipe served as a mini speed bump, and into the parking lot. Wyatt and Jack leapt from the still-moving car and sprinted up to the front door as Hardin threw the car into park and quickly joined them. A brief check of the parking lot and surrounding area revealed no people and no other cars, including the hearse. All three men stood at the front entrance, unsure of what awaited them inside.

They readied themselves for a struggle, but there would be none on this day. Wyatt put his hand on the doorknob and slowly gave it a twist. The door was unlocked.

Ω

Omega had already set up the makeshift burial plot, having had some of his men dig the four-feet-deep hole and erect the stainless steel device used to lower caskets into the ground. He whirled the hearse around and backed up near the large dirt pile that would be used to refill the hole. He popped the back door and then reached into his black bag for the syringe containing epinephrine. He tapped its sides to clear any air bubbles and carefully uncapped the needle. His hands had a slight tremor, shaking with the anticipation and excitement of the moment. Peeling back the lower half of the coffin's lid to expose the two women's legs, Omega picked out a target site. A smooth, fluid push and the needle pricked its way through Heather's skin and into her left calf muscle. The same steps were rapidly and immediately repeated with Annette. Before the medication had begun to work its magic on the women, he slammed the lid shut and tugged the casket onto the guide rods, where it came to rest against the end stop. The nylon straps underneath grew tighter as the weight of the coffin rested against them and hugged the side rails. Omega wheeled around and released the hand brake of the lowering device, allowing gravity to sink the hefty casket deep into the grave. Hurriedly, he disassembled the steel device, slid it into the hearse, and clambered aboard a Bobcat earthmover he had stashed nearby. It was only a matter of minutes before he had pushed all the dirt from the freshly dug hole back into its previous home. He shut off the motor, leaving the earthmover for his employees to pick up later, and leapt back into the cab of the hearse. It was time to move. Atlanta was calling.

28

The three men entered cautiously through the front door, guns drawn. Agent Duvall led the way, followed closely by Chief Hart, with Detective Barnhill bringing up the rear. They fanned out in different directions, each sounding out an all-clear in his specific room. No one in the reception area. No one in the chapel. No one in the storage area. No one in any of the offices. There was no sign of the owner and operator of this place, Hank Klayman. The men advanced slowly through the opposite door and back outside. They circled around the corner of the building and found Klayman's SUV parked in the rear, camouflaged in an old shed containing some excavation equipment and various other items used in the funeral business. The hearse was missing.

"He's gotta be at the graveyard!" puffed Duvall.

"Fits right in with the taphophobia," Wyatt reasoned.

Immediately, the three doubled back and blazed out of the funeral home parking lot in the direction of Pine Knoll Cemetery.

$$\Omega$$

The women awoke to a vaguely familiar yet very different sound. At first, it sounded like brief rumbles of thunder, followed by intermittent rain showers. Maybe they'd fallen asleep watching TV and a thunderstorm had knocked out the power. The blackness enveloped them like a blanket—it was almost … smothering. And there was the sound again! What was that?

Heather tried to roll over, but something was preventing her from doing so. Had she fallen asleep on her arms and made them feel heavy?

She wiggled her fingers and felt … more fingers! Fingers that weren't her own. Her brain lurched and shook itself out of its fog as she began to focus and think more clearly. A low moan crept from behind her, startling her momentarily. Annette! Heather tried to twist her head but still was unable to move. The feeling had reentered her arms. Leaning her shoulder forward, she nudged something soft and cushiony, like a pillow.

Annette suddenly jerked behind Heather, and another low-pitched moan rose from her throat.

"Annette?" Heather whispered.

"Heather?" Annette returned.

"Where are we? Are you okay?"

"A little groggy. And I can't move my arms!"

Annette attempted again to move her arms, which were handcuffed behind her back. As she wrenched her wrists, Heather's hands joined with hers, moving together in synchronicity.

Heather cried out in pain. "We're stuck together! I think I feel rope."

"No! Handcuffs!" Annette wailed.

"Oh my God!"

There was the noise again—a thump and clatter—and then a small cloud of dust filtered its way into the coffin, causing Heather to sneeze.

"God bless you," Annette said automatically.

"Thanks," Heather said, her voice trembling. "Annette, we really need to pray. We are in some big-time trouble!"

"I know! It's gotta be Omega!"

"I think he's burying us alive! Those strange sounds—I think Omega is shoveling dirt on us!"

"Oh my God!" Annette shrieked.

"Sh-h-h!" Heather cautioned. "We have to conserve oxygen. We're gonna have to calm down if we want to make it out of here alive."

"But what if we don't?" Annette cried.

"We can't think like that. We've got to breathe slowly and steadily. If we do that and stay positive, we'll make it. We need to calm our nerves and not talk too much. It'll use up the air faster. Besides, I'm not ready to see Jesus just yet!"

That thought made the hairs on both of their arms stand on end, in spite of the sweltering heat.

"Let's just say a short prayer," Annette suggested. "Then I'll just pray in my heart."

"I will be too, sweetie."

The two alternated their prayers. Annette went first and prayed rapidly.

"Lord, be with our husbands and guide the search and rescue teams. Be with Heather and me. Give us a calm spirit in this claustrophobic situation. Help us face our fears and defeat the evil one. Whatever happens, may Your will be done, Lord."

After a second or two, Heather began.

"Father, give us peace and protection," she quickly spoke. "Help us to hold onto You and Your promise to never leave or forsake us. Keep Annette calm. Keep me calm. Jesus, may You alone be glorified though this. Amen."

Heather and Annette squeezed each other's fingers as they said amen and then became silent as they tried to still their own rapidly beating hearts, hearts that thudded so loudly that they could hear them beating in their ears. Their body position was uncomfortable at best, but any wiggling would mean one less breath of air for later, and at this point, every breath counted. They would have to fight off the pain of their cramped quarters. Their very lives depended on it.

$$\Omega$$

Wyatt had radioed to all law enforcement officers in town to be on the lookout for a suspect, possibly the Omega Killer, driving a hearse. He and Agent Duvall hastily ordered roadblocks at all routes leaving Valley Springs. The killer's identity and description would soon blanket the police band like a winter blizzard. Henry Lee Klayman. White male. Late fifties to early sixties. Slim build. Salt-and-pepper hair.

Several of the other officers had arrived at the funeral home as Hardin, Wyatt, and Jack raced for the cemetery. Duvall directed them to wait until a search warrant had been issued before they swept the premises more thoroughly. Once it arrived, they tore the place apart, dismantling everything, inside and out, in hopes of finding any evidence that would incriminate Klayman. Unfortunately, they found nothing.

$$\Omega$$

The man known as Henry Lee Klayman—Hank to most of his friends in Valley Springs but now currently exposed nationally as the Omega Killer—was on the run. At least, he wanted everyone to think he was. Determined to outsmart his pursuers, he'd driven the hearse out to the municipal landfill near the outskirts of town and ditched it behind a huge mountain of trash. The scent would throw off the tracking dogs while he escaped on foot. He jogged two or three miles into the nearby woods, where he'd constructed an elaborate hideout in the foundation of an abandoned house that had been destroyed by a tornado decades ago.

He had set up a nearly broken-down casket-lowering device around a sinkhole that had formed where the front porch once stood. Stretching out flat on the nylon webbing straps, he kicked the brake release with his heel and gradually lowered himself into the sinkhole. He swept away a strategically placed broken tree branch, revealing a small ventilation grate in the side of the concrete wall. A slight tug and the grate popped off rather easily. He grabbed the tree branch and reached up to rake the lowering device into the pit. He quickly dismantled it and tossed the steel pipes and fittings into the hole in the concrete. Klayman slithered, like the snake that he was, through the opening and then replaced the grate. Sunlight streamed in through the small slots in the metal. He let his eyes adjust to the difference in light and then reached for one of the many oil lamps he'd stored in this concrete bunker. He'd worked diligently in stocking the bunker over the past several months. He would use natural sunlight during the day and lamps at night. Cases of water lined one of the walls, enough to last for several months. A radio with batteries was on a small shelf nearby. Food staples, such as beef jerky, crackers, sunflower seeds, granola, canned fish, canned chicken, fruit cups, and other nonperishables, were wrapped in heavy plastic bags to keep out any wild animals. He had a huge duffel bag filled with such toiletries as soap, toothpaste, toothbrushes, disposable razors, pain relievers, deodorant, wet wipes, and toilet paper. He would take care of his bodily functions by using empty water bottles and utilizing a small latrine he had dug not too far from the sinkhole. The cover of darkness would serve as the perfect time to take care of these personal hygiene matters. Night would also serve as the best time to bathe in the creek that ran just a few yards west of his new shelter. He would be able to wash his clothes in the same stream every few weeks or so. He'd stashed enough changes of clothes under the house's foundation to last for nearly fourteen days. An old army cot would serve as his bed. He had everything he ever needed right here. He was the king of his castle, even though his castle was a hole in the ground—somehow very fitting for a funeral director. It would work until all this blew over in a few months. Then he could sneak into the big city under an assumed name and wreak more havoc than Atlanta had seen. It would be a long wait, but for Hank, it would be well worth it.

Ω 29

For what seemed like the umpteenth time in the past twenty-four hours, the three men were roaring away in Duvall's car, chasing what possibly could be the end of their story: the apprehension of the perpetrator responsible for multiple heinous crimes against the good people of Valley Springs. This time, however, there was a search-and-rescue twist. They'd figured out his game, and now they'd have to hope and pray that they could find the girls before it was too late. The men knew that Heather Barnhill and Annette Hart had been buried alive somewhere. Logic pointed them toward the cemetery. They were going on a hunch. They prayed that they were right. Jack Barnhill was nervously talking his way through the particulars of the killer they'd first known as Omega, now known to them as Hank Klayman.

"It all makes sense now. He was always the one in school and in church who seemed to have more than a little doubt about his faith. It seemed like he wanted to believe, but every argument or discussion ended in his playing devil's advocate," said Jack.

"Literally," fired Wyatt, hardly able to control his anger.

"Hank was always a little weird, but I just thought it was because of all the dead people he had to be around every day," Jack went on. "That's why he left red omega symbols on the index cards. He was quoting Jesus, quoting Scripture in his own twisted way."

"Revelation 22," Hardin offered.

"Right, and the unlucky thirteenth verse on top of that. Perfect for someone with a God complex—someone who wants us to face our fears on *his* terms, not God's."

"Say it again for me," requested Wyatt.

"I am the Alpha and the Omega, the First and the Last, the Beginning and the End," Jack quoted.

"He was the end for most people in this town," Wyatt said. "As funeral director, there's no telling how many people he's buried. He's the last one to see them before they're covered up with dirt. There's no telling how many times he's heard that particular verse too. Gotta be grating on his nerves, since he's not a believer."

"Is he usually the one they call from the hospital when a patient has expired?" questioned Jack.

"Well, yes. Why?"

"So the hospital staff, nurses, doctors, and pharmacists think nothing of his roaming the halls. He's just there to pick up another body. No one questions him. He's on a first-name basis with nearly everyone. Basically, he has no problems with security clearance. He can come and go as he pleases. He's one of them."

Wyatt nodded and finished Jack's thought. "Hank had unfettered access to the pharmacy. No one would ever question him about being back there. That means he would be able to sneak out midazolam and epinephrine with no problem at all. He'd have access to medical files on the computers at the nurse's stations, so he'd know the diagnosis of everyone who'd been admitted to the hospital or the emergency room. A doctor's computer password would gain him access to the files at that particular doctor's individual practice. An all-access backstage pass. Brilliant."

"And he wouldn't have shown up on the medical professionals list!' Jack said. "He was totally flying under the radar. Who would suspect him?"

"No one," Wyatt concurred. "That's why he's been able to get away with as much as he has."

Hardin took the next corner a little too fast, causing the tires on his sedan to squeal and the other two men to slide in their seat. Each one gripped the handle attached to the roof as they careened up the hill toward the entrance of Pine Knoll Cemetery. Adrenaline and a large dose of fear fueled their brains as they tried to think of where Hank might have buried the women.

"Sorry, guys," said Agent Duvall. "Trying to get us there faster."

"In one piece, please," remarked Wyatt. "Don't get us killed."

Jack shot a sideways glance at Wyatt, alarmed at his poor choice of words.

Wyatt lowered stared at his feet in embarrassment as he realized what he'd said, but Hardin intervened.

"Keep your eyes open, gentlemen. We're looking for plots that look freshly dug. Obviously, there've been several funerals in the last couple of weeks, so we're looking for the one that looks like the dirt's just been repacked into the hole."

"Should we split up into quadrants or stay together?" Jack asked.

"I think we should stay together. There can't be more than three or so newer grave sites," stated Wyatt.

"I agree," said Hardin. "If anyone would know, Wyatt, it's you. We stick together on this one."

They quickly pulled through the brick entrance to Pine Knoll Cemetery. The old graveyard had been around since the 1850s, but the caretakers had done an incredible job of keeping it well manicured and free from vandalism. It had no fence to surround its borders, but there were several signs posted nearby, declaring that visitors were only allowed during daylight hours. The entire population of Valley Springs knew of the sunrise-to-sunset rule, and most were respectful in following the practice. However, a certain funeral director had recently broken the edict, under cover of darkness, by stashing an earthmover in a strategic spot for later use. Now his hired hands had come to collect it, presumably after a recent funeral. The flatbed truck had been backed up to a small clearing not too far from the burial plot. One of Klayman's workers had cranked up the Bobcat and was turning it around so that he could drive it up the ramp that the other man had lowered to the ground. Once they'd driven it onto the flatbed, they'd run the chains through it to hold it down, drive back to the funeral home, and call it a day. But Hardin, Wyatt, and Jack had other plans in mind for these men. Jack was the first to see the two men loading the earthmover onto the truck.

"Over there! Over there!" he shouted.

"Got it," Hardin shot back, steering through the maze of headstones and bouncing the car down the dirt path toward the northeast corner of the cemetery. He hit the brakes with both feet and slid the car to a stop some thirty yards from the truck. Each of the law enforcement officers unclipped his holster but did not draw a weapon. They carefully crept up to the men, the workers only giving them brief glances as they busied themselves with the earthmover.

"Chief, you want this?" whispered Agent Duvall.

"Yes, sir. I'll take it. I know these guys."

Wyatt slowed his pace a little more and moved out even farther toward the middle of the dirt path. Never losing his charming Southern accent, he got directly to the point. "Hey, Willie. Hey, Ernest. Y'all doing all right?"

"Yes, sir. Yes, sir. We're doing good," Willie returned.

"Which one of these graves was the last one you guys dug?"

"The one right behind us," Willie said, jabbing his thumb over his left shoulder. "That one over there is Ms. Watson's"—he gestured over Wyatt's head with an index finger—"and old lady Caldwell is right there, between here and Ms. Watson. I'm not sure who this might be. Someone already filled in the grave before me and Ernie got here."

Wyatt's pulse spiked and he shot a glance at Jack and Hardin. "Do you still have the backhoe here with you?"

"No, sir. It's back behind the funeral home. Mr. Klayman told us to come out here and get the Bobcat. It's right here if you—"

"You got shovels in the truck?"

"Yes, sir. Probably four or five of 'em."

"Willie, we're gonna need you and Ernest to give us a hand."

"Yes, sir. Anything. What do you need?"

"Bring the Bobcat back down from the flatbed. We've gotta dig up this hole."

"But Chief Hart, isn't that disrespectful to the dead?"

"Willie, whoever's in that casket down there may not be dead!"

Willie's eyes grew as big as saucers. He could hardly speak, but stammered an agreement to help. Then he signaled to Ernest to remove the chains and drive the earthmover off the back of the flatbed. While he rolled the heavy machinery down the ramp, Willie jogged back to the truck and produced four shovels.

"The Bobcat won't dig down very far. That's what the backhoe's for," Willie replied matter-of-factly. "Shovels are gonna be our best bet, even though they're very slow."

"Four shovels are better than one," said Agent Duvall. "We can move faster this way. I don't think we have the time for you guys to get the backhoe down here again."

Ernest steered the earthmover toward the grave at Willie's instruction and then gradually began to scrape away at the layers of dirt. Time seemed to crawl, especially for Wyatt and Jack. They could do nothing but watch as bucketfuls of dirt were scooped out of the hole until finally, the Bobcat had reached the maximum depth of what it could do, and their shoveling could begin.

Ω30Ω

It was hot, humid, and musty. The woman lay in the darkness, drifting in and out of awareness. Each one's thoughts morphed from prayer to sleep and back to prayer again. Their clothes were beginning to smell with the odor of stale sweat. Their bodies had perspired profusely and then dried in the smothering heat that made them drowsy. The cycle seemed to repeat itself every fifteen minutes or so, causing them to go from sweat-soaked chills to hot flashes. The loss of body fluids made their mouths as dry as the dirt encasing their casket. Neither one could remember the last time she swallowed easily. Both women's calf muscles were achy and starting to cramp up, partly from the needle stick that Omega had given them. They tried flexing and relaxing their toes against the end of the casket wall. It provided some temporary relief, but since there was no way to adjust their bodies, the cramps soon returned. Still, their husbands had taught them the importance of keeping their mental clarity when in an untenable predicament. The mind could keep a person alive, despite physical limitations. As long as a person was thinking clearly and not in a panic, chances of surviving and overcoming adversity were much greater. A calm attitude and a confident spirit were the keys to success. That and a lot of prayer.

$$\Omega$$

Hank Klayman had rested peacefully, stretching out on his army cot like a cat sunning itself on a warm spring day. He knew the sun would be going down very soon and that any possible search for him would be over until the morning. He didn't want to stray too far, but he decided to take a short reconnaissance mission, stretch his legs, and use the latrine. He'd scout the outlying area to see if anyone was on his trail and think about what his next move should be—and when he should make that move. He checked his watch. 7:45 p.m. He'd grab a quick bite to eat from his stockpile of nonperishables and then go on the prowl, as soon as the last remnants of daylight ducked behind the horizon.

$$\Omega$$

Dusk had crept its way into Pine Knoll Cemetery, and Ernest had done all he could possibly do. The excavation was in full swing, and the three officers and Willie had began to spade out shovelfuls of sediment from each corner of the rectangular-shaped pit. The normal depth of a burial plot was around four feet or so, depending on the person's size or undertaker's preference. If they worked nonstop, the four men could possibly have the pit dug out in an hour or so.

"You got any portable floodlights in your car?" Jack asked Hardin.

"Great idea. I'll get those set up right now," Hardin replied as he jumped out of the hole and made a beeline for the car's trunk. Within five minutes, he had set up the staging, hooked up the portable generator, and powered up the lights. The steady humming of the generator served as background noise to their huffing and puffing as they continued to plunge their spades into the earth. A heightened sense of awareness swept over the men each time a shovel struck something solid, but the culprit would turn out to be either a large rock or compacted clay that had turned hard under the southern Georgia sun. They tried not to think of the worst-case scenario, choosing to focus on their digging and the unbridled joy they would feel once the girls had been found. A few other officers had just arrived on the scene, some ready to take on any crowd control measures that might arise and to provide relief for Jack, Wyatt, and Hardin. The men were starting to get winded, and all of them had rings of sweat that soaked through their clothes. Jack and Wyatt knew that time was not on their side, so instead of trying to be heroes and refusing to give up their shovels, they willingly handed them off to a couple of the younger, newly arrived agents—men who were fresher and could dig for a longer time would help speed up the process and possibly be the difference between life or death for Heather and Annette. Hardin was the last to give up his shovel, tossing it to an underling who looked to be at least twenty years his junior. The men kept checking their watches, realizing the time crunch that they were under. After fifteen more minutes of digging, which seemed like hours to the men who were now watching from Willie's truck, the agent who had taken Jack's place at the lower left side of the hole called out to his superior.

"Agent Duvall! I've got something here!"

The man's shovel swept away the small crumbles of soil with his hand to reveal the corner of a casket.

$$\Omega$$

Thump!

They'd both been hearing scratching noises for a few minutes, but this particular noise was different.

Thump!

The two women strained to see in the darkness. The air was so thick and heavy that they were unable to cry out. But somebody—or something—was out there, making a loud noise.

Annette managed to croak weakly, "Hello? Hello?"

Every ounce of strength seemed to have been sapped from their bodies. The heat and humidity was so unbearable that all they wanted to do was sleep. But that sound was out there, and it wouldn't go away.

Thump!

Their minds were still alert, but their bodies were just … so … exhausted.

$$\Omega$$

Wyatt, Jack, and Hardin found their second wind and sprang from the tailgate of Willie's truck. They dashed over to the grave and snatched the shovels away from the younger men. Agent Duvall began to carefully carve around the outline of the coffin as the other two men raked at the top of the once-shiny surface. Willie continued to plug away at the lower right-hand corner, steadily revealing the other edge of the casket. He knocked on the lid but could hear no response over the portable generator.

Jack furiously worked the blade of his shovel into the red Georgia clay, tossing clods of thick mud out of the hole. Another four or five inches down, he finally reached the lid and began to scrape all over the top of it. Wyatt jumped in and assisted Jack at the same spot, quickly revealing the ornate trim that ran along the top and sides of the casket. He tried yanking on the coffin's lid. Nothing. Still partially buried.

$$\Omega$$

Heather could hear it—the soft drone of a motor. Her eyes widened as she concentrated on the direction and the volume of the sound. "Do you hear that?" she asked Annette. *We can't be buried very deep if we're hearing these noises*, Heather thought.

"M-m-m ... I heard ... something," Annette replied groggily.
Tap. Tap. Tap. Tap. Tap. Tap. Tap. Tap.

Annette gasped. "But I know I heard that!" she exclaimed. Both of the women tried to sit up, but their bodies were crammed into much too small a space, not to mention the agonizing cramps they'd been suffering. They'd also forgotten that they were still handcuffed together.

"We've gotta get their attention!" Heather cried.

"Can you move your legs at all?" asked Annette.

"I ... I think so."

"On the count of three, we're gonna do a scissor-kick together. Kick your top leg up toward the lid. With any luck, whoever's out there will hear us."

The two women summoned up their courage and took one last deep breath.

"One …two … three!"

The women threw their legs up against the cushioned lid. The top didn't budge, but dust and dirt spilled through the cracks, making them cough. They waited, but heard nothing.

Outside, Wyatt spied the pieces of sand, rock, and dirt flying toward his face. He flinched and then began to shout. "Something's moving down there! The top of the coffin just popped up! I think … I think they're alive!"

Jack and Hardin joined Wyatt in the hole, digging with their fingers under the edge of the lid, scratching at the last vestiges of clay holding the casket underground. Someone was down there, and they prayed it was the two women they'd been looking for all day. The women for whom they would gladly trade their lives.

Ω 31

Hank Klayman had walked down to the creek that carved its way through the forested area surrounding his new home. He'd spent a few hours scouting the outlying woods, taking mental notes and bringing his adrenaline rush under control. It was quite peaceful, this far outside of town, but the trees were full of all sounds. The noise of chirping crickets, cicadas, and small birds filtered through the thick pine branches. Leaves rustled, owls hooted, and small animals scurried back and forth across the forest floor. Klayman paid these creatures no mind. He was deeply lost in thought. The anticipation and allure of Atlanta pulled at his soul like a young child tugging on his mother's overcoat. The waiting was the most difficult part, but it was much too risky for him to make that move now. Every branch of law enforcement, from the locals all the way to the FBI, was on the lookout for him. He had to lay low and he knew it. The waiting was just so hard. His mind was on the things to come, the dreams of the big city, even though his body was stuck in the present, in the backwoods of Valley Springs. He inhaled another large breath of fresh air, exhaled, and closed his eyes. It was almost time for him to catch a few winks. Daylight was on its way.

$$\Omega$$

The hunter sat in his deer stand, motionless except for the blinking of his eyes. He'd been perched on the seat for several hours now, surveying the world from twelve feet in the air. So far, he'd seen nothing. Rusty Thomas slowly ran a hand across his face and down through his bushy mustache and beard. He was worn out, and with the sun trying to peek over the horizon, he knew his chances at bagging a whitetail deer were evaporating by the second. *I'll wait one more minute and then I'm outta here*, he'd told himself. No sooner had the words entered his brain than a movement suddenly worked its way into the corner of his eye. His peripheral vision was excellent, and he knew immediately what it was. An eight-point buck eased its way into the clearing, turning its head from side to side and sniffing the air. Rusty's pulse spiked as he watched the deer's stop-and-go movement. The buck bent his neck to munch on something on the ground. Rusty raised his gun and peeped through the scope of his .30-06 hunting rifle. He reasoned that the animal was between 250 and 300 yards away. Rusty slowly and steadily positioned the rifle against his shoulder, sighted the deer once again, took a deep breath, and fired. The deer reeled from the blast and then darted for the woods to its right. Rusty hurriedly made his way down the ladder of the deer stand and made a beeline for the clearing. He'd shot the large buck! The easy part was over. Now came the hardest part: tracking down the beast.

$$\Omega$$

They'd already summoned two emergency services vehicles to Pine Knoll Cemetery in anticipation of finding Heather and Annette alive. Now, the four paramedics watched as Hardin, Wyatt, and Jack continued to claw at the clay around the coffin's edges. One of them ran back to the rig and brought back two crowbars, handing them off to Wyatt and Jack. After a few more minutes, they were able to wedge the crowbars under the lid.

As the men leaned the whole weight of their bodies into the crowbar, the lid groaned and creaked and finally cracked, sending the hinges and part of the top splintering away. The floodlights poured into the small opening as Jack wrenched off the rest of the casket lid. The sight shocked, horrified, and thrilled him all at once—two bodies lying back to back, caked in sweat and red dirt. But breathing! Alive! They were alive!

"Annette! Heather! Can you hear me?" Jack shouted as he looked over at Wyatt. Both of the women wiggled their fingers and tried to open their eyes, but after being in the dark for so long, the slightest flicker of light was like staring into the sun. They squinted and turned their heads away from the spotlights.

"Jack? Is that you?" Heather mumbled, hope welling up in her voice.

"We're here, babe. Hold tight. We're gonna get you out."

Wyatt produced a pocket knife and began to saw away at the strands of nylon rope that had dug deeply into their wrists and rubbed them raw in the process. He yelled back at no one in particular as he worked at the ropes. "I need some bolt cutters here! We've got ropes and handcuffs!"

Several men scurried away to retrieve the cutters. Heather and Annette continued to lay perfectly still, the sides of their torsos still rising and falling with every breath. It was a welcome and unique scene, different from what they had grown accustomed to with Omega. Jack and Hardin continued to deconstruct the rest of the casket so that the paramedics would have easier access. After the ropes had been cut, Wyatt snapped the chain linking the handcuffs like a twig with the newly produced bolt cutters. The first inclination of the women was to jerk upright and get out of the coffin, but Wyatt gently reassured them to stay put.

"Don't get up, ladies. Stay still. We want to make sure everything's okay with you, physically speaking," he said, unable to take his eyes off Annette. He leaned down and quietly whispered to his wife. "Hang in there, sweetie. I love you."

"Love you," Annette mouthed dryly.

A short time later, the sounds of wood and fiberglass splitting apart were music to the ears of everyone around the scene. The coffin had been filleted and exposed on every side. The two women were gently rolled onto their backs as the EMTs dropped into the hole with stretchers right behind them. Heather was lifted out first and an oxygen mask immediately strapped over her mouth and nose. As they began to check her vital signs and start an IV to rehydrate her, the second group of paramedics hoisted Annette out and performed the same procedures with her. A short time later, the women were stabilized enough to be loaded into the back of the two waiting ambulances for transport to the hospital.

Hardin spoke up. "You boys go with your wives, but keep your cell phones on. Come back when you feel like everything's okay. I'll let you know if anything else breaks. I've got all the routes out of town still blocked, so I can assure you he's not driving out. We're getting some men on the door at the hospital for you and the girls."

Jack and Wyatt expressed their thanks, climbed in the back of the emergency vehicles, and sped away.

They were still within view when the cell phone in Hardin's pocket rang. He checked the caller ID. "What's up, Hayden? Kinda covered up here, so make it fast."

"Just making sure you got the gift I sent you."

"The gift?"

"Yes, and I hope that DVD is my ticket for an exclusive—"

"Well, it's helped us get much closer to solving this thing, so thanks for the tip."

"Word is, you guys are chasing him down right now."

"Like I said, we're close. I've got your back on the exclusive, but keep it quiet for now. I don't want this thing jeopardized for any reason."

Ω

The blood drops were spaced out at regular intervals every few feet, a deer hunter's version of Hansel and Gretel. Rusty followed the trail of red dots over the leafy underbrush. He'd tracked the deer for at least a mile or so, pausing every once in a while to look through the scope. No movement, but he was getting closer. His boots were caked with mud from a recent thunderstorm, so he had to be careful where he walked. As the blood dried, it would become darker and almost match the color of the mud, making it that much more difficult to stay on the trail. He rounded a bend and dropped down into a small hollow that fed into a short clearing. The clearing backed up to a shallow creek that gurgled quietly in the early morning hour. The sun had already risen, so it wouldn't be long before the deer would seek refuge under the shade of the trees. He followed the blood across the creek and up the bank before he produced the scope again. Scanning the forest floor, he spied the deer bounding through a thicket and scampering farther away. As he watched the deer through the scope, something else caught his attention. Off to his right, Rusty saw a concrete foundation of what once might have been a house. A single retaining wall and maybe an old front porch. It was hard to tell for sure what it used to be. But what was that? A foot? Something—or someone—appeared to be crawling through a small hole in the side of the concrete. A large tree branch lying on the ground suddenly slid over and covered the hole. The scene stopped Rusty dead in his tracks. Who was living out in the middle of the woods? In the middle of nowhere? *Some homeless person*, he reasoned. But there were no homeless people to speak of in Valley Springs. *Another hunter?* A hunter wouldn't hide under a porch. It was too strange. He suddenly forgot about the deer and turned to make his way back toward his truck to retrieve his cell phone, double-timing it across the woods and hoping that this wasn't a wild goose chase he was about to phone in to the already overworked police department. He'd already given up on his deer. He didn't need the attention of public ridicule to add insult to injury.

32

The FBI was on his trail, but he was firmly entrenched in his concrete cubbyhole. Hank Klayman had lived in Valley Springs all his life. His parents had reared him as most parents in this area did. They'd gone hunting, fishing, hiking, and camping during his formative years, so he was used to being in the great outdoors. It was a vital part of his being. He knew how to set up and maintain a hideaway, especially when he'd had months to scout and prepare it. To him, it was just an extended camping trip, a time to find himself before he moved on to the next phase of his life. But for now, he had to lay low. He'd done some scouting overnight and watched as the sun sneaked its way over the horizon and through the trees. His eyes were starting to droop, and his energy was beginning to wane. Since he'd reversed his sleep cycle, his body was starting to revolt against itself. He knew he'd need a couple of days to get his circadian rhythm back to a sense of normalcy, and now was as good a time as any to get that process underway. There was something strange about going to sleep at ten in the morning, but nothing in Hank's life would ever be normal again—although he was totally oblivious to that fact. In his mind, he was simply helping the Lord do His work. The part that failed to sink into his thick skull was the truth of the matter: the Lord didn't want or need his help. Jesus only desired his obedience, and that was something Hank refused to acknowledge or to give. For now, all he wanted to obey was his longing for sleep. He stretched out on his cot, pulled the blanket up to his neck, and gave in to the heaviness that rapidly consumed him.

Ω

They'd sped to the hospital and quickly wheeled the ambulance through the emergency room drive-up. A team of doctors and other medical personnel met them at the door and hurried them into a waiting critical care unit. Jack and Wyatt stepped to a corner of the room as a flurry of activity swirled over and around the wives. Fresh oxygen in large tanks was administered, along with additional IV fluids. The doctors checked hearts, lungs, head and necks, torsos, and all extremities. Halfway through the examination, they had been escorted from the room by a well-meaning nurse as one of the doctors shined a penlight into one of Heather's eyes. After a short protest and promise that they would soon be let back into the room, the men trudged to the waiting area, where they plopped into two vinyl chairs that had seen better days. The silence was deafening, as neither man spoke, each concerned about the health of the women inside. What seemed like an eternity passed before one of the ER physicians emerged from behind double doors and moved in their direction. Both men stood in anticipation.

"Gentlemen, you don't know how lucky you are—or how lucky *they* are," the doctor pronounced. "For women who were buried alive, I'd say they're in remarkably good shape."

"So, they're gonna be all right?" asked Jack.

"They'll be fine in a few days. We're going to admit them into the hospital for observation. Both are severely dehydrated, but that's to be expected, and that's something we can easily fix. They inhaled dust and dirt that we're trying to clear out of their lungs. They have some nasty lacerations around the wrists and ankles, a few bruises, but nothing major. Overall, I'd say they're very, very lucky."

Jack and Wyatt exhaled and thanked the doctor profusely.

"When can we see them?" asked Wyatt.

"We're moving them to a private room shortly, and I understand they'll be under extremely tight security. Is that correct?"

"Yes, sir. These women are the only survivors and possible witnesses to a serial killer."

"Amazing! They should buy a lottery ticket with that kind of luck."

"The Lord had His hedge of protection surrounding them. It's a testament to the power of prayer, so I'm not sure how much luck had to do with it. It was the hand of God, if you ask me," the chief replied.

"We're going to put them down at the end of the hall in rooms 134 and 135, so if you need time to get your security detail set up, we should be wheeling them down there in an hour or so."

"Will do. Thanks again, Doc."

The doctor pushed his way back through the doors of the critical care unit, shaking his head in disbelief, and checked on the women once again. He'd never seen anything like it in all his years as an ER physician. Maybe prayer really did change things.

$$\Omega$$

Rusty Thomas hopped into the cab of his pickup truck and fired the engine. He'd slung his hunting rifle on the passenger-side floorboard and snatched up his cell phone from the center console. He dialed up the Valley Springs Police Department as he put his truck into gear and made his way back toward town. The dispatcher picked up after the second ring.

"Valley Springs Police Department."

"Hey, Sara. This is Rusty Thomas."

"Hi, Rusty. How can I help you?"

"Listen, I was out hunting on some land between Highway 28 and the dirt road that runs parallel to Longleaf Road. I was tracking a deer I'd shot when I ran across—or at least I *think* I ran across—a man out in the woods."

"You *think*?"

"Yeah, he was crawling underneath the foundation of an old house."

"Rusty, are you positive you saw someone or do you just *think* you saw someone? We don't have time for this today. Don't you know we're trying to find—"

"No, I don't *think*. I *know!* I know what I saw! It wasn't another hunter, but it was somebody. And since we don't have a lot of homeless folks in this town, I think—"

"Was it someone camping?"

"No, he wasn't camping. He was just crawling under the foundation or maybe down into the basement."

"And where were you again?"

"The woods that border 28 and Longleaf Road."

"Okay, we'll send a car out there as soon as we can. It may be a while, with all this Omega stuff, but I'll have someone ride out there and take a look."

"But don't you think it could actually *be* Omega?"

"I doubt it. I think he may be long gone."

"What makes you so sure?"

"Listen, Rusty. We're doing the best we can under the circumstances. Keep your cell phone on in case we need to get in touch with you. Now I've gotta keep this line clear, so I'm gonna have to let you go. We'll get out there in a little while. Thanks for the tip."

"Okay," Rusty said half-heartedly. "Let me know what you find."

"We will. Take care, Rusty."

"Bye, Sara."

Rusty slammed down his cell phone in frustration. He wasn't crazy. He wasn't drunk. He was most definitely not imagining things. Somebody was out there, and he suspected that it was the man everyone else was looking for now.

$$\Omega$$

Jack sat in the hospital room, gently holding Heather's hand as she slept. His lifelong friend, Wyatt, was next door, doing the same with his wife, Annette. His feelings were an odd mixture of contentment and concern—content that his wife was okay physically, but concern for Wyatt, the burden on his shoulders, and just how quickly everyone could get this case solved so that Klayman could not do this to anyone else. Jack let his mind wander as his eyes drifted to the television mounted high in one corner of the room. He could hear the news anchor through the tiny bedside speakers, going on about the Valley Springs cases. Everyone seemed to have an opinion or a solution that would magically apprehend the perpetrator and end the madness, once and for all. Jack had to giggle, if only a little, at the so-called pundits who probably hadn't worked a crime scene in more than twenty years, if at all. *If it were that easy, then why aren't they doing it instead of flapping their gums on TV?* he thought. After a few more minutes of mind-numbing drivel from the talking heads, Jack's eyes became heavy. It had been a long day, and now it was starting to catch up with him. He let his eyes close for only a second and then they refused to open. His catnap was awakened by a firm but gentle hand on his shoulder. Startled, he jerked his head upward. Wyatt was staring at him.

"Just got a call from Duvall."

Jack looked around groggily, trying to figure out exactly where he was. His brain desperately craved sleep and was starting to shut down on him. The brief nap only seemed to make it worse. He stared blankly at Wyatt, as if he were a stranger, trying to connect the dots, trying to wake up.

"Jack!"

Jack finally recognized his surroundings, and it all started to make sense. The hospital. Heather. His best friend, Wyatt. "Yeah, what's he got?" Jack croaked.

"They found the hearse. It was abandoned at the back of the county landfill but no sign of Klayman anywhere."

"Hmmm, no shocker there."

"Hardin's sending an FBI helicopter to run a thermal imaging scan over a five-square-mile area, just in case he's on foot, but I personally think that horse is out of the barn."

"Maybe, but Hardin must be on to something. He wouldn't have called us to come in for that."

"You okay with leaving our wives right now?"

Right then, Heather startled the men by snapping out of her slumber long enough to croak her response. "Annette and I will be … highly ticked off … if you don't get out of here … and do everything within your power … to bring that … monster to justice."

Ω 33

Wyatt and Jack managed to weave their way through traffic, dodge reporters stationed outside police headquarters, and duck in through the back entrance of the building. Hardin was inside, nervously pacing back and forth across the tiny conference room, waiting for the pair to arrive. He had a Styrofoam coffee cup seemingly glued to his right hand. He sipped absent-mindedly as he listened to the others on the team dissect the evidence they'd gathered about Klayman. Most of the commentary was being provided by Agent Spikes of the GBI, who was expounding on the significance of the abandoned hearse. The conversation had definitely tipped in his favor as he explained the law enforcement side of things to Doctors Brown and Sheffield. Agent Duvall was content to let Spikes do the talking, as it gave him more time to piece together what they did have. He snapped out of it as Wyatt and Jack barged into the room.

"Hey, fellas. How are your wives? Give us a quick update," Agent Spikes said as he abruptly stopped his previous dialogue.

"They're fine. Cuts and bruises. A little dehydration. Lungs have some dust and dirt in them, but for the most part, they're fine. They'll make it," Wyatt explained as everyone made their way to a chair. Everyone sat down, but Hardin's nervous energy caused him to pop up and pace again as he laid out their game plan.

"Okay. We've got forensics sweeping everything Klayman owns. The hearse. His personal vehicle. His home. Anything that'll give us a clue. The last thing we know about him is that he abandoned the hearse over in the landfill. We're not sure if he's left the city, but—"

He was interrupted as the door to the conference room swung open. It was the day-shift dispatcher, clutching a phone message in her hand. Sara made a beeline for her boss, Chief Hart. She leaned down and whispered to him. "Sorry to interrupt, but we just got this call-in from a hunter and I didn't know if you wanted to check it out."

"Who's it from?" Wyatt asked.

"Rusty Thomas."

Chief Hart gave her a stern look and then gazed down at the message. His brain suddenly lurched into gear. "His hunting land is over near 28 and Longleaf, isn't it?"

"Yes, sir."

"That's only a couple of miles from the backside of the landfill."

"Is this anything you guys would care to share with the group?" Hardin asked, sounding a little like an old schoolteacher.

"Sara took a message from a local hunter saying that he might have seen someone out in the woods a few miles from the county dump."

"Well, if that's the case, we'll know soon. I've got birds in the sky running thermal imaging programs. If he's out there, we'll get him."

"That property is heavily wooded, and it backs up to the landfill. There are a couple of abandoned shacks out there. People used to live in them years ago, but I think a tornado wiped out most of the livable parts of the houses."

Jack jumped into the conversation, obvious concern in his voice. "Don't you think we should set up a perimeter around the woods? If he's in there—"

"That's an awfully big *if*," interrupted Hardin.

"True, but if you think about it, it makes perfect sense. He ditched the hearse at the edge of the woods. The scent of the landfill would mess up the dogs, so that would make it darn near impossible to track him that way. He'd only have a short jog into the woods to set up camp near one of the old shacks."

"Thermal imaging would pick him up, Jack."

Sara spoke up unexpectedly and awkwardly out-of-turn. "Rusty said that the person he thought he saw was crawling underneath the house."

"Can thermal imaging pick up diffused heat through a concrete wall?" fired Jack.

"Not likely," returned Hardin.

"So we've got a fugitive on the run, hiding in a dense forest, possibly in a concrete bunker of some kind. Thermal imaging will never find this guy."

"How about the basement angle? Not many houses out there, so which ones have basements?" chimed Wyatt.

Light bulbs went on in the brains of everyone in the room.

Suddenly, Hardin started barking out orders. "We need to pull up an old map or some old geographic or topographic images. We can set up a perimeter around the woods, but only send specific teams in to search the old houses. Agent Spikes, coordinate the perimeter setup. Use your boys from the GBI and the local enforcement teams."

"Got it," Spikes confirmed, immediately dialing up the reserves from his cell phone.

"Dr. Brown, can you help us out with those maps? I know it's not your area of expertise, but if anyone knows this town, it's you. I'm gonna need Chief Hart with me, so I need you to run with this one."

"I'm on it," Brown declared and dashed out of the room.

Just then, Agent Duvall's cell phone began to buzz silently with a text message from his helicopter patrol: NO HUMAN IMAGES PICKED UP IN THE FOREST.

Hardin sent his thanks and told his pilots to stand down for now. "Jack, you're right. My pilots just sent me a text. They found no human images. That means it's very possible that he's hiding in one of those houses or at least in an old cellar. Let's get that perimeter set up. Then when Dr. Brown gets the maps out to us, we'll storm the houses. We'll go in teams of three. Jack and Wyatt, you guys stick with me. Dr. Sheffield, be ready to talk to this guy. If he's out there, we're bringing him in. He'll be a perfect case study for you. All right, let's get out there!"

Ω

Hank Klayman continued to snooze, oblivious to the impending storm that would soon engulf the town of Valley Springs, in general, and him, specifically. He rolled over and pulled the blanket over his head to shut out the small rays of sun creeping into his basement home. He breathed deeply and sank into the relative comfort of the thin cot mattress. Then he began to snore.

$$\Omega$$

Within the hour, a virtual convoy of police cars was cruising toward the dirt road bordering the woods that ran the length of Longleaf Road. A roadblock was starting to take shape as the officers parked their cars on the shoulder of Highway 28. Once all the available patrolmen had arrived on the scene, a command post was set up and led by Agent Spikes. He poured over the square mileage of the area and then rapidly calculated the distance to fan out each individual policeman so that the entire acreage Klayman was thought to be in would be surrounded. Spikes radioed each checkpoint thirty minutes later to make sure that everyone was in place and had their weapons drawn. Soon after, a black van weaved its way around the roadblock and rolled up next to the command post. The van's door slid open and nine FBI agents—in full tactical gear and armed to the teeth—lumbered out. They would be on standby until Agent Duvall could get there with the digital maps. He was the agent in charge of the whole operation, so no one moved or did anything without his authorization.

$$\Omega$$

The three men and Dr. Sheffield rode in silence down Highway 28 toward the landfill. The only thing that broke the deafening quiet was the wireless portable fax machine that jolted to life and spat out the maps that Dr. Brown had tracked down during his research. His fact-finding mission had led to the rediscovery of three abandoned properties in the nearby area. Hardin tried to pinpoint the three targets while attempting to maneuver around the roadblock and get to the command post. Once he'd managed to safely park the car, he debriefed two of the tactical teams on how he wanted to handle the approach on the sites. He designated the third FBI team as a backup, in case something went terribly wrong. As he prepped the other two FBI teams on how he wanted Klayman taken down, should they stumble upon him, Jack and Wyatt suited up in Kevlar vests, goggles, and helmets. Along with Hardin, they would comprise the third team. The first team would track down the northernmost property, the second team would take the area directly to the east, and the third team would take the land due south. They would move in tandem, leaving at the same time and reporting back only if they found Klayman. Agent Duvall checked in one last time with Agent Spikes. "Agent Spikes, is our perimeter secure and ready to go?"

"Ten-four. We are a go. Ready on your command."

"Team one, you ready?"

"Yes, sir. We're ready."

"Team two?"

"Ten-four. Ready and steady."

"Jack? Wyatt?" Hardin whispered off-mike.

"Ready on your call," Wyatt said.

"Let's get him," said Jack.

Duvall said a quick prayer before he gave the go signal. "Dear Lord, please help us. We need You. We can't do it without You. We're putting this mission in Your hands and totally trusting You with it."

"Amen," Wyatt and Jack both agreed.

Then with a wave of Duvall's hand, they were off.

Ω 34

Team one headed north along the dirt road and then took a hard right down through a winding maze of pine trees. They followed an overgrown deer path deep into the woods, moving stealthily so as not to make a sound. The GPS guided them around a hill and over a small stream before they saw it—an old burned-out clapboard home sat directly in front of them. The home rested on four large stacks of cinder blocks that formed a column at each corner, so there was no visible basement. The team could clearly see all the way under the house and through to the other side. At this vantage point, they were approximately fifty yards from the front door. The team leader immediately snapped his men into formation, radioed in to the command post, and then stormed the old rotting shack. One of the men bounded up the concrete steps and onto the wooden porch, almost falling through the decaying boards. The other two had circled around back, found no rear door, and made their way back to the porch to cover the team leader as he crept inside. They shoved their way through the front door, weapons drawn. Once they were all inside, the team scattered in different directions, each one eventually sounding out an "all clear." They searched the dilapidated house from top to bottom, even searching for trap doors under the floor. No sign of Klayman. The team-one leader radioed back to Agents Spikes and Duvall.

"Team-one leader. North property is all clear. Repeat. North property is all clear."

"Ten-four, team-leader one. Stand by for instructions."

Ω

Team two made a beeline directly east. They had the farthest distance to travel among the three groups, so they were double-timing it across the forest floor. The team-two leader kept a careful eye on the GPS, but they were still some distance away. The pine trees were tall and bunched together, casting shifting shadows on the ground below and making it seem darker than the hour would indicate. The men were focused and alert as they bounded over several hills and through a huge clearing. The clearing seemed out of place in such a thick forest, until they saw the giant pile of trees that had been pushed to one end of the area. Beyond the pile, they saw the large concrete slab. This was it! The men crept slowly in formation until they'd reached the slab. But that was all that there was. Nothing but a concrete slab where a home must've stood several years ago. Team two circled the slab and its surrounding perimeter several times to no avail. Nothing. No one there or nearby. This was a definite dead end. The team-two leader called it in to Agent Spikes.

$$\Omega$$

Hardin and the rest of team three could hear the verdicts of the other two teams over their earpieces. Wyatt and Jack exchanged a nervous look as they heard the all-clear call from team two. At this point, there could only be two possible outcomes. The first: team three was on the trail of Hank Klayman and was about to bring him to justice. The second: Klayman had somehow eluded them.

Hardin held up a hand to stop, adjusted his goggles, and checked the GPS. Less than half a mile to the target. Team three slinked along the edge of the creek, looking for any other kinds of clues. Footprints. Burned-out campfires. Anything that might give a hint as to any other human possibly inhabiting these woods. They approached in a triangle formation, with Agent Duvall at the point. Jack's heart pounded in his chest as his mind flipped through all the potential scenarios. He tried to concentrate as his eyes swept from left to right. He was positioned to the right of Duvall, his field of vision spanning the length of the tree line on the right. Wyatt was to Jack's left, his coverage encompassing the entire tree line on the left side. They inched closer toward the target before Duvall threw out his right arm. Team three stopped as one. Duvall pointed to his left, and the team sloshed its way across the cold, shin-deep waters of the winding creek. They climbed up a small rise and angled left. Then they saw it, right along the edge of the tree line. The remains of a home left to rot in the dense undergrowth. The only thing left standing was part of what had once been the back wall of the house and the foundation itself. As they prepared to search the area surrounding the home, they discovered a sinkhole in front of them. *Probably where the front porch used to be,* Hardin thought. Cautiously peering down into the pit, they noticed that the foundation of the house had not vanished. It was completely intact, as well as a basement or crawlspace situated underneath it. Jack and Wyatt fanned out to the corners of the sinkhole as Hardin eased onto his backside and dropped in. He edged over to the concrete wall, nudged a fallen tree branch to one side, and peeped through the ventilation grate. Hardin couldn't see very well into the darkness below, but he could hear something. Snoring! It was Klayman! He turned and whispered into his microphone. "It's him. He's asleep under the foundation in the basement."

Every eye widened back at the command center. They snapped to attention, waiting for their orders.

"Can you see him?" Wyatt asked.

"No, but I know it's him. I can hear him breathing down there. He's asleep and he's snoring."

"So, what now, boss?" chimed Jack.

"We're gonna flush him out. It's too dangerous for us to go in and get him. He might have this place booby-trapped." Hardin lost himself in thought for a few seconds, the silence chilling both Jack and Wyatt to the bone. "Martin, tell your boys to close in to one mile from our site. Team one and team two, set up a perimeter behind us at five hundred yards. Do not move in on Klayman unless you hear from me. You've got fifteen minutes. Move out!" Duvall moved the microphone away from his mouth, climbed out of the hole, and motioned Jack and Wyatt over. "Okay, here's what we're gonna do. Shake, shock, and smoke Mr. Klayman out of his little hiding place. We string together two concussion grenades with two smoke canisters and two tear gas canisters. We lower them in through the grate on the side of the basement. We set it on a two-minute timer and then detonate it. If the concussion doesn't stun him enough, the smoke and tear gas will send him running for fresh air. There's only one way out, and he's *gonna* have to come out. When he does, we'll be ready and waiting. We take him alive, no matter what. No questions asked. It's not ours to administer justice; it's ours to bring him to justice. I trust that you two can handle that, despite what you and your wives have been through. If you can't, step away right now."

Both men stared at him, neither one daring to move an inch.

"Okay, good. Let's bring him in."

The three men put their years of knowledge and experience to use, stringing together the canisters, the grenades, and the detonator in virtually no time at all. Duvall pulled the microphone back down to his mouth and checked in with Spikes. "Agent Spikes, your team in place?"

"We are a go, sir. Ready when you are. Good luck, sir."

"Thanks. Be ready in case something goes wrong."

"Ten-four."

Team three stood in front of the sinkhole, taking in the enormity of their situation. Inside, their adrenaline was flowing and their hearts thumped through their chests. Mentally, they were all making a concerted effort to relax and slow down their breathing. Duvall swallowed hard and looked over at Wyatt. "You wanna do the honors?"

"Yeah, I'll do it."

"All right, here's how we set up. Jack, you'll be in the hole on my right, facing the grate, which will be on your right. Wyatt, once you lower the package inside the wall, you'll take your position opposite Jack. You'll be on my left and facing the grate, which will be on your left. I'll be above you outside of the hole, directly in front of the grate. Any questions?"

Jack and Wyatt shook their heads and readied themselves for the impending operation. Wyatt gently lowered the rope, carrying the homemade device to Jack, who'd already jumped into the sinkhole. He looked over at his lifelong friend and arched his eyebrows.

"This is for our girls," Wyatt mouthed.

"For Annette and Heather," Jack replied, giving him the thumbs-up sign. Jack backed up two steps, dropped to one knee, and hunkered down in the corner of the pit. Hardin readied his rifle and then got into a comfortable shooting position. Wyatt peered over his shoulder and received the okay sign from Duvall. He crept over to the grate and gently popped it off with a utility knife. He slowly eased the device into the concrete wall, being careful not to clink the canisters together and give Klayman any kind of advanced warning. Finally, he pressed the timer, pulled the pin, and quietly replaced the grate, readying himself next to the wall for the upcoming storm. Time seemed to stand still as the men waited for the two minutes to tick away. Sweat began to roll down Jack's forehead as he continued to try to keep his heart from leaping out of his chest.

The explosion of the concussion grenade echoed against the cement, snapping team three to attention. A short time later, smoke began to pour out of the grate in huge puffs. Not long after that, the grate flew away from the wall like a bullet, and a coughing, gagging Hank Klayman dove through the opening in search of fresh air. He found fresh air, but he also found something else: his old friends from team three.

Ω 35

Coughing violently and desperate to catch his breath, Hank Klayman didn't realize what was happening until it was too late. Out of the corner of his eye, he spied a pair of black boots pointed in his general direction. It only got worse as he lifted his head to see two rifles aimed directly at him. They'd flushed him out! He dropped his head and continued to clear his lungs. His eyes burned from the noxious gas as well as the reintroduction to daylight, forcing him to squint just to see anything at all. He'd try to plot his next move, but at this moment he was stuck. He was like a beached whale frantically trying to force air into his lungs. The others watched him in amazement, feeling both overly cautious and amused at the same time. When Klayman finally gathered his bearings, he spoke as the man they'd previously known only as a voice over the telephone. The familiar tone of Omega.

"What are you guys trying to do? Kill me? That's not very nice." Klayman slowly straightened up, his thumbs hooked through the loops of two grenades hanging from the sides of his cargo pants. The sight caused all three of the other men to tighten their aim on him. A grin slowly spread across his face as they stared him down. "Easy, fellas. Easy does it. You wouldn't want me to pull these pins out, would you?"

"Keep your hands where we can see them!" barked Agent Duvall.

"I'll show you my hands but trust me, I don't think you want me to raise them. We'll all go boom."

"Hank, how could you do this? Why would you resort to *this*—to these murders to get your point across?" asked Wyatt earnestly.

"Well, it's like this, Wyatt, ol' boy. When people say one thing and then live their lives totally to the contrary, well, let's just say it drives me nuts. Back in our younger days, I was always shunned for being a doubter, a questioner of the truth. But at least I was honest. At least I was true to who I really was within my soul."

"And where did that get you?" Hardin interrupted from atop the pit. "Staring down the barrel of three automatic weapons, that's where."

"Ah, dear Agent Duvall. I wouldn't speak so smugly and so loudly if I were you. You can't even muster up the courage to tell your brother about the 'love and amazing salvation power of Jesus. Why won't you be honest with him? Isn't he looking down the same gun barrel, figuratively speaking? All you are doing is proving my point. Your Bible says that you are supposed to 'go and make disciples' of everyone. What's the matter, Hardin? You afraid of your own flesh and blood? Afraid of what he'll say to you or if he'll make fun of you? Report you to your superiors? Apparently, honesty is *not* your own best personal policy."

"This is not about him, Klayman! This is about you!" shouted Hardin.

"Oh, but that's where you're wrong. What about his decision to throw our friends Jack and Wyatt under the bus? All that stuff bounces back and splashes up on you. That's not very Christ-like, letting him run amok and allowing him to get away with trampling the reputations of your Christian brothers. You could make this right, but you don't, because you're scared of your own brother. Your own *twin* brother. Suck it up, man! Face the truth! Face your fears!"

"That's enough!" Wyatt thundered.

"Shut up, Wyatt! I'm not talking to you right now! I'll get to your transgressions shortly. Right now, I'm exposing Hardin for the fraud that he really is."

"Hank, you of all people—"

"I said *shut up*, Wyatt! I swear I'll pull these pins!"

"Relax, Hank. It's okay. It's okay," Jack said softly. His soothing voice calmed the frazzled nerves of everyone involved in this odd standoff. "You don't want to do that. You don't want to kill yourself or anyone else, for that matter."

Hank roared with laughter. "I'm not trying to kill myself, Jack. And I won't kill you guys, unless you get in my way. I'll tell you what; let me talk to you for a minute, Jack. These other two knuckleheads seem to be more interested in talking *at* me than listening *to* me."

"You've got a captive audience, Hank. Let's talk. I'm all ears."

Hank let out another belly laugh. "I like you, Jack. Lots of spunk, just like our high school days. You know, I never got that condescending attitude from you, even back then. You've always treated me with respect, and I appreciate that."

"Thanks."

"That being said, you stand in my way. I'm on a mission, and you're keeping me from carrying it out."

"Hank, I hate to disagree with you again about this, but I think you need to hear it. Apparently it's not sinking in."

"I know, I know. It's not my place. God doesn't need any help moving things along. I'm not performing a public service. Blah, blah, blah. I heard you. I got it."

"No, not that. Sounds like you already know that anyway. What you need to hear is that Jesus still loves you and wants a personal relationship with you."

"I'm not interested in your proselytizing! This is hardly the time or place for it! You need to listen to what *I* have to say! I tried to warn people that they need to practice what they preach. Don't sit in church and smile at me when I've seen you out at bars getting drunk, or cheating on your spouse, or working late to earn more money at the expense of time spent with your family. Hypocrisy! Everybody's a 'Christian' when it's convenient for them or when they get into some kind of trouble. Everybody's a 'Christian' on Sunday, but how about the rest of the week? Or when no one else is looking? If that's what your faith is based upon, I'm glad I rejected it. Those people have turned faith into nothing more than a religious exercise. There *is* a big difference in faith and religion, and I never want to be a part of that culture. I noticed it first in middle school and even more in high school. I had to … I had to teach those people a lesson. And if I couldn't teach them a lesson, I'd go for the one person that would hurt them the most. A spouse. A child. It didn't matter. Whatever would truly turn their hearts to Jesus … or harden it like mine."

"So why did you come after Heather and Annette?"

"You know, girls can be so cruel in middle school. They ridiculed me, not because I was funny-looking or a geek—the normal reasons middle-schoolers do what they do. They made fun of me because I wouldn't accept Jesus on blind faith. I had a lot of questions, and no one wanted to give me any answers or defend their beliefs. They just basically said accept Jesus as your Savior or you're a freak, doomed to burn in hell. That's not exactly showing the love of Christ, is it?"

"Hank, they were just young, excited kids. They were new in their faith, new in their walk with Him."

"Yeah, well some wounds don't heal over time, Jack. They become scars, and most people don't go for other people with scars! They ostracize them. Make them feel … unwanted, unloved. Scars are permanent, Jack."

"Everyone's scarred to a certain extent, Hank. Sin ravages the hearts of everyone, including Christians. It scars our lives, our hearts, our relationships, and the lives and hearts of those around us. But the scars don't have to be permanent. There is One who bore the scars so that we don't have to. He died on a cross to wipe away our scars. You've just gotta trust and believe in Him, not some religious ritual or misguided saint."

"No! It's too late for that! I've already gone down this road, made too many bad choices, and I can't turn back. Now it's time I paid the fiddler. Too many people have died because of me, so what's a couple more?" Hank had lulled them into thinking he was about to commit suicide. Instead, he lifted his hands in surrender, pulling the pin from each of the grenades. He dropped the one in his left hand first, and it landed at his feet.

He was trying to kill Wyatt and Jack. Hardin took his eyes away from Hank for a millisecond. "Get outta there!" he screamed at Wyatt and Jack from atop the pit. As the two men scrambled and dove out of the sinkhole,

Hank lobbed the other grenade directly at Hardin. Hardin instinctively put his hands up to deflect the flying object and then rapidly took cover behind a huge pine tree.

Wyatt dove head first to his right and covered his head with both arms. Meanwhile, Jack leapt up to his left and rolled out of the hole onto his right shoulder. He tucked his head down and came up quickly on his knees. He saw Hank boot the first grenade away and try to follow him out of the pit. His years of training and instinct kicked in at the same time the adrenaline did. Jack jerked his weapon toward the head of Hank Klayman.

And fired.

Time seemed to move in slow motion as the two grenades detonated at the same time as the gunshot, sending showers of dirt, rock, and chunks of pine tree in every direction. Seconds later, the dust settled and the scene slowly came to life. Jack raised his head and peered across the pit. His best friend, Wyatt, was lying face down, unmoving. He ducked down and tilted his head to the left. He could see Hardin hunkered down behind a tree, alive and well, calling in the other teams over the radio for reinforcement. But where was Hank? Jack eased his head up once again and looked straight ahead. He could see Wyatt start to stir a bit, trying to push himself up from the forest floor. Edging closer to the pit, Jack peeked inside. Lying next to a huge crater caused by the grenade explosion was the body of Hank Klayman. His eyes were closed. All of his body parts were still intact, but he was covered in rubble. Jack strained his vision, desperate to see if the man was still alive. A quick jerk of his head in Hardin's direction and a thumbs-up sign flashed in return sent both men scurrying toward the hole. Crawling on all fours, they eased into the overgrown grave and checked Hank's pulse. He lay on the ground face up, his head tilted slightly to the right. A huge welt the size of a lemon and already turning bright red and purple had sprung up near his left temple, courtesy of the rubber bullet fired by Jack. Hardin crept up beside Hank and felt his carotid artery for a sign of life. He turned and nodded to Jack. Still alive.

Just then, Wyatt staggered up and slid over to their position. "He gonna make it?" he asked, not exactly knowing which answer would make him feel better.

"I think so," answered Hardin. "He's got a nasty knot on the side of his head, and right now he's unconscious, but he'll be okay. Jack really blasted him from close range, so it's gonna sting for a while."

"It's a good thing we swapped out the real bullets for the rubber ones." Jack smiled as the other two FBI teams and various emergency personnel swarmed the scene. "Even a rubber bullet will put a hurting on you from less than ten feet away."

"I wanted him alive, not dead. I want him to pay for everything he's done and everything he's put the good folks of Valley Springs through. Death would've been the easy way out for him, and I wasn't gonna let that happen. He's gonna stand before that judge and take his punishment like a man, and I hope the sentence is more than harsh. Then he'll see just what it's like to face his fears," Wyatt said.

The three men exchanged knowing glances as a grin slowly crawled across each of their faces. They sat on the edge of the missing foundation as the paramedics attended to their minor injuries. They had nothing more than bumps, bruises, cuts, and a slight ringing in their ears from the grenade detonation. Other than that, they were perfectly fine. The same couldn't be said for Henry Lee Klayman. Once the medical personnel had brought him to and administered basic treatment, he was shackled by his arms and legs to the gurney and lifted out of the hole. As he was wheeled by the three law enforcement officers, they happened to catch a glimpse of his eyes. Not surprisingly, they were flat, dull, and unblinking. He offered no smile, no smirk, or no scream, just a lifeless expression attached to a living body. He said nothing but stared straight into the sky, straight into the face of God, as he was loaded into the ambulance and driven to the hospital. It was over. Hank Klayman's twisted world was no longer relevant. Omega's reign of terror had officially come to an end.

Ω 36

Two weeks had passed since the FBI made the announcement that had rocked the nation. They'd apprehended the most notorious serial killer of the modern era. The Omega Killer was in federal custody, awaiting trial on several counts of murder in the first degree. He wasn't the most brutal serial killer in terms of blood, guts, and gore, but he was definitely the most cerebral. He was the very definition of premeditated murder, his motives no less pure than the most crazed slasher. The prosecuting attorney had promised to go for the death penalty, but Klayman had hired one of the most well-known defense attorneys in the country, one who'd made his reputation and his fortune defending mob bosses. He'd been pushing hard for life without parole, so far without much agreement from the Feds. In the Feds' opinion, there was too much collateral damage in terms of victims and their families to settle for giving Klayman life inside a taxpayer-funded prison.

As for the "collateral damage," the four survivors of Klayman's swath of terror were getting better day by day. Nick Wayne, Annette Hart, Heather Barnhill, and the boyfriend of the 9-1-1 operator were nursing their minor physical injuries and receiving counseling for any mental trauma. All the while, they were counting their blessings, fully aware that they'd been fortunate to have survived the ordeal. They were living proof that prayer still worked, and God still performed miracles.

$$\Omega$$

Hardin Duvall and his twin brother, Hayden, had made a deal of sorts. Hayden had used his contacts with TVBN to slip inside the hospital and gain access to the pharmacy's security tapes—the very same DVDs he'd slipped anonymously to Valley Springs Police and had made their way into the hands of Dr. London Brown. The DVD had been the key piece of evidence in discovering the identity of Omega and would surely be invaluable during the upcoming trial. Hayden had subtly let it be known that he wanted to break the news of the killer's arrest when it happened, and Hardin had seen to that. Now there were more deals to be made.

"Look, if I can slip you more exclusive stuff on Klayman before we go to the rest of the national media with it, will you do one thing for me?" asked Hardin.

"Absolutely. What is it?" Hayden replied.

"I want you to go to church with me this Sunday."

"You want *me* to go to church with *you*? That's it?"

"That's it."

Hayden gave his brother the strangest of looks before he responded with a stunned chuckle. "Yeah, I can do that."

"No backing out now. I'm giving you a good deal here."

"I promise. This Sunday. No backing out."

"Good."

$$\Omega$$

Wyatt spent the vast majority of his two weeks racing between the police station and his home. It was extremely important to make sure all the i's were dotted and t's were crossed on Klayman's case. He didn't need any kind of loophole or crack tiny enough for Klayman to slip through and somehow earn a premature release. When he wasn't at the station being Chief Hart, he was at home being Wyatt to his recovering wife. Annette was receiving counseling, and it helped her psyche to know that her husband was there for her and that her best friend, Heather, was going through the exact same situation. Sometimes, just being there to hear her story and help her deal with the mental and emotional side of the matter was almost better than any other kind of counseling. It was the best thing for her emotional well-being at this point. She, like Heather, would eventually be okay. Healing the emotional scars would take time, and the vast majority of them would go away. But the innocence, the invincibility, and the trust that a small town once provided—those things were gone. It would be a while before she and Heather could build up that trust again with the town of Valley Springs. However, it was their hometown, and they would learn to love it again. It would just take a little time. God and time.

$$\Omega$$

Heather and Jack walked down the dirt road, hand in hand. The red clay crunched under their feet like a thick layer of snow. Neither one said very much as they walked. They seemed only to want to soak in the scenery, to reminisce about days gone by. Days of innocence … and innocence lost. Everywhere along the horizon, as far as they could see, there were no indications of the chaos that Valley Springs had just endured. The corn still grew tall and green out in the fields. The cotton, soybeans, and peanuts burst from the ground in leafy bunches. Highway 28 ran perpendicular to the dirt road, stretching out like a snake in front of them. The pecan trees swayed and creaked in the breeze. The pine trees stood straight and tall, like sentinels guarding the bright blue sky. Various small animals scurried through the fields and ditches bordering the dirt road, dodging the birds that swooped low in search of an easy meal. Some things in this part of the world hadn't changed since Heather and Jack had walked this very same road as high school sweethearts. Then again, some things had.

"So, where do we go from here?" asked Jack as he gently tugged Heather toward the highway intersection.

"Well, how do you still feel about moving here?" she returned.

"I'm still all right with moving here. I want to live here if you do. We've just got to get the plans together for getting the house built. The thing is, we can't spend our lives living in fear or constantly looking over our shoulders. That's no way to live. Then again, I haven't lived through what you've lived through. If we let fringe lunatics like Klayman affect the way we live our lives, then he's accomplished what he's set out to do."

"Yes, but Valley Springs just feels … different now. It used to be so idyllic, so peaceful and serene. Innocent. Now I'm not so sure."

"Valley Springs is still the same town. The vast majority of the people haven't changed, and that's what Valley Springs really is in our minds."

"But wasn't he trying to change the people of Valley Springs, based on what he was seeing from them?"

"Remember, this guy wasn't the most mentally stable person in town, so I'd take his warning with a grain of salt. We all sin. We all fall short of the glory of God. It's not his job to point that out. He had his own set problems to deal with before he could even think about tackling anyone else's."

"There's just something missing now in Valley Springs. It's like he stole its innocence."

"No, he's proven that we live in a fallen world, and even a small town is not immune to that. It makes us realize that we need to cling to Jesus even more now than ever before. We've got to be the ones to take the first step. We can't be pushed by someone else to do it. We've got to depend more on Him and less on ourselves, if we truly want to live without fear."

Heather sighed and leaned on Jack's shoulder as they walked on. She knew he was right, but it wasn't easy watching her image of Valley Springs melt away like an ice cube in the sun. Their silent jaunt was disturbed by a cell phone ring. Jack reached into his pocket, fished out the phone, and glanced at the caller ID—Atlanta Police Department. He switched the phone to vibrate. He'd take that call later on. Right now, all he wanted to do was enjoy a Saturday evening stroll with his bride.

Ω

"Hey, Jack, this is Jerry. On behalf of the Atlanta Police Department, I wanted to call and congratulate you on a great job in solving the Omega cases. Agent Duvall told me what an asset you were in bringing the perp to justice. He's also pulled some strings here, and as chief of police, let me be the first to tell you that your retirement is now official. You won't have to serve out the few remaining days you had left. Congratulations again! You make us proud. Call me when you get this message. Talk to you soon. Bye."

$$\Omega$$

Pastor Noel Marshall was not one to exploit a tragic situation such as this, but the opportunity was there, and he would be remiss not to take advantage of it. The Lord had pressed it on his heart to seize the moment. In light of the Valley Springs murders, he'd never seen his church pews so full. Everyone was still scared and searching for answers. They needed love. They needed reassurance. They needed comfort. He would give them all of these, but he would also give them what they needed most of all: the Truth.

"The past few weeks in Valley Springs have been eye-opening, to say the least. It has given us all a wake-up call, reminding us that, even though we live in a small town, we are not as insulated from the evil things of this world as we would like to believe we are. It has awakened us to our own mortality, and that makes us uncomfortable. We are in need of healing, both spiritually and emotionally. Our nature, our sin nature, is such that we already have our minds made up about Hank. Our thoughts probably run along the lines of 'Let's fry him, and get things back to normal.' Make no mistake about it. He deserves to be severely punished. *I* want to see him punished, and I know you do as well. He should face the stiffest possible sentence the judge and jury will allow, and I believe he will. One question I must ask you is this: will we ever get back to normal, and do we even want to go back to the way things were? Think about your life, your *spiritual* life, before Mr. Klayman scared us out of our wits. Take a spiritual inventory. Now, are you totally satisfied with your daily walk with Christ? In the words of the corporate world, do you meet expectations, exceed expectations, or are you in need of improvement? Only you can answer that question, but you need to plumb the depths of your heart and soul. Be honest with yourself. Did Hank have a point? Don't misunderstand me. I'm not sympathizing with him at all! Please hear me on that. I'm merely asking you how your daily walk is going. Only when we are where we should be as Christians can we ever hope to know how to react to all this chaos! Let me be transparent with you for a minute. One of the biggest things I personally struggle with as a Christian is forgiveness. Yet the Word tells me I am to forgive others as He has forgiven me! And I think to myself that this is too fresh, too raw, too heinous an act. I can never, ever forgive this man for what he's done to these families, this town, and my friends! But my Savior commands me to. I'll be honest. I'm not ready to forgive him right now. It's gonna take some time for me, as it will for most of you. It hurts. It hurts badly. Matthew 6:14–15 pretty much spells it out. Jesus will forgive you when you sin *if* you forgive others when they sin against you. And Matthew 18:35 says you have to mean it with your heart. So if we truly desire to live our lives as Christ intended us to, we've got to depend on Him to give us the strength and a Christ-like attitude of the heart to eventually forgive this man for the vile things he's done. Just like Jesus has forgiven us for all the vile things we've done. What will you choose? Obedience? Or holding a grudge as if it was your best friend? This is your time to draw nearer to Christ. Will you?"

Jack and Heather sat hand in hand, nestled in the back right corner of the church, unable to control their tears. There was hardly a dry eye in the sanctuary on this particular Sunday, including Wyatt and Annette. They sat on the same pew, just to the right of Heather, so that both women were able to hold each other's hand as well as her husband's hand. Hardin and Hayden Duvall had slipped in with Dr. London Brown and settled on the back row directly behind the Barnhills and Harts. They would often rest a comforting hand on the shoulders of those in front of them as the pastor continued his sermon. The service seemed to be part grieving, part repentance, and part revival. Clearly a lot of pent-up anxiety and emotion found its way to the surface of many in the congregation, something that had been long overdue in coming. As many people prayed at the altar and many more prayed from the relative comfort of their pew, the sun beamed even brighter through the church's stained-glass windows. It was a day of healing. Healing of hearts. Healing of minds. Healing of emotions. Healing of souls. They'd been through the fire, and had become stronger and more refined in the process. One day—and one day soon—this town would be able to smile again. God was already beginning to smile down on them, and the days ahead would only get brighter.

CPSIA information can be obtained at www.ICGtesting.com
Printed in the USA
LVOW130856260613

340206LV00005B/6/P